SYDNEY HARBOR HOSPITAL: EVIE'S BOMBSHELL
by Amy Andrews

The biggest questions on everyone's lips revolve around
legendary heart surgeon Finn Kennedy and tough-talking
ER doctor Evie Lockheart. Now these questions are
finally answered as their chemistry reaches fever pitch!

And if you've missed any of the stories in our fabulous
Sydney Harbor Hospital series,
why not go back to where it all began?

Dear Reader,

Ever since the *Sydney Harbor Hospital* series hit the shelves, readers have been asking for Finn and Evie's story. And I can't blame them, because I have to admit to more than a passing fascination myself as I wrote their subplot in Mia and Luca's story. But I just kept thinking, *there's no way Finn can be redeemed—it'll never be done. I pity the one they ask to do that.*

And then they asked me to do it…gulp!

But in all honesty I was ecstatic to be chosen, because I'd already written a prequel for Finn and Evie quite a few months prior—their very first meeting—so I've been invested in their HEA for a while, and I do so like a challenge….

But how do you redeem a man who's as emotionally shut down as Finn? Evie's been trying for years to reach him with no success. Well, it wasn't easy. I had to strip him right back and throw a huge curve ball at him, and then have the one person he's always counted on subconsciously to be there, despite his perennial bad mood, walk away.

Yep, Finn was a tough one—but Evie was tougher. She refused to take his scraps, demanding all of Finn. Demanding the fairy tale. Refusing anything less.

And she got it, too.

I hope you enjoy their journey to Happy-Ever-After-land.

Amy

SYDNEY HARBOR HOSPITAL: EVIE'S BOMBSHELL

Amy Andrews

HARLEQUIN® MEDICAL ROMANCE™

This book is dedicated to all the loyal Medical™ Romance fans who always look for our books and love a good series!

ISBN-13: 978-0-373-06880-7

SYDNEY HARBOR HOSPITAL:
EVIE'S BOMBSHELL

First North American Publication 2013

Copyright © 2013 by Harlequin Books S.A.

Special thanks and acknowledgment are given to Alison Ahearn for her contribution to the *Sydney Harbor Hospital* series.

This edition published by arrangement with Harlequin Books S.A.

For questions and comments about the quality of this book, please contact us at CustomerService@Harlequin.com.

® and TM are trademarks of Harlequin Enterprises Limited or its corporate affiliates. Trademarks indicated with ® are registered in the United States Patent and Trademark Office, the Canadian Trade Marks Office and in other countries.

H HARLEQUIN®
™ www.Harlequin.com

Printed in U.S.A.

Recent titles by Amy Andrews

HOW TO MEND A BROKEN HEART

SYDNEY HARBOR HOSPITAL: LUCA'S BAD GIRL*

WAKING UP WITH DR. OFF-LIMITS

JUST ONE LAST NIGHT…

RESCUED BY THE DREAMY DOC

VALENTINO'S PREGNANCY BOMBSHELL

ALLESANDRO AND THE CHEERY NANNY

*Sydney Harbor Hospital

**These books are also available in ebook format
from www.Harlequin.com.**

PROLOGUE

EVIE LOCKHEART BELTED hard on the door, uncaring if the whole building heard her. Loud rock music bled out from around the frame so she knew he wasn't asleep. 'Open up now, Finn Kennedy,' she yelled, 'or so help me I'm going to kick this fancy penthouse door right in!'

She glared at the stubbornly closed object. It had been two weeks since he'd been discharged from hospital after the less than stellar success of his second operation. Two weeks since he'd said, *Get out. I don't want you in my life*. Two weeks of phoning and texting and having one-sided conversations through his door.

And it was enough.

She was sick of Finn shutting her out— shutting the world out.

And if she didn't love him so much she'd just

walk away and leave him to rot in the cloud of misery and denial he liked to call home.

But memories of the infection he'd picked up after his first operation and the state he'd got himself into as he'd tried to self-treat were never far from her mind and she was determined to check on him whether the stubborn fool wanted her to or not.

She was about to bash on the door again when the lift behind her dinged and Gladys stepped out. She'd never been happier to see Finn's cleaner in her life.

'Gladys, I need Finn's key.'

The older woman's brow crinkled in concern as she searched through her bag. 'Is he all right? Is he sick again?'

'No,' Evie dismissed. Gladys had found Finn collapsed on the floor overwhelmed by his infection and still hadn't quite got over the shock. 'He's probably fine but I'd like to see it with my own two eyes.' *Then I'm going to wring his neck.*

Gladys stopped her frantic search. 'He was fine yesterday,' she hedged.

Evie had to stop herself from knocking the dear sweet little old lady, who also happened to clean her apartment along with many others at *Kirribilli Views*, to the ground and forcibly searching her bag.

'He told you not to give me the key, didn't he?'

Gladys looked embarrassed. 'I'm sorry, Evie. But he was very firm about it.'

Evie suppressed a scream but she stood her ground and held out her hand. 'Gladys, I'm begging you, one woman to another, I need to see him. I need the key.'

Gladys pursed her lips. 'You love him?'

Evie wasn't surprised that Gladys was in the gossip loop, given how long rumours about she and Finn had been floating around Sydney Harbour Hospital and how many of its staff lived at Kirribilli Views. She nodded, depending on the incurably romantic streak she knew beat inside the old cleaner's chest.

'Yes.' Although God knew why. *The man was impossible to love!*

Gladys put her hand in her bag and pulled out a set of keys. 'He needs someone to love him,' she said, holding them out.

'He needs a damn good spanking,' Evie muttered, taking the keys.

Gladys grinned. 'That too.'

'Thanks,' Evie said.

'I'll leave his apartment till last today,' the elderly woman said, and turned back towards the lift.

Finn glared at her as the door opened and Evie felt the glacial chill from his ice-blue eyes all the way across the room, despite the darkened interior from the pulled-down blinds. 'Remind me to sack Gladys,' he said as he threw back the amber contents of a glass tumbler.

Evie moved towards where he was sitting on the couch, noticing how haggard he was looking. His usual leanness looked almost gaunt in the shadows. His regular stubbly appearance bordering on scruffy. His dark brown hair messy as if he'd been constantly worrying at it with agitated fingers. The light was too low to see the streaks of grey that gave him that distinguished arrogant air he wore so bloody well.

How could a man look like hell and still cause a pull low and deep inside her? And how, *damn it all*, could he stare at her with that morose belligerence he'd perfected and still not kill off her feelings for him?

Finn Kennedy was going to be the death of her. God knew, he'd already ground her pride into the dust.

The coffee table halted her progress and she was pleased for the barrier as the urge to shake him took hold. 'You're drunk.'

'Nope.' He poured himself another finger of Scotch from the bottle on the coffee table. 'Not yet.'

'It's three o'clock in the afternoon.'

He raised his glass to her. 'I appreciate this booty call, but if you don't mind I have a date with my whisky glass.'

Evie watched him throw it back, despairing how she could get through to him. 'Don't do this to yourself, Finn. It's early days yet.' She looked down at his right arm, his lifeless hand placed awkwardly on his thigh. 'You need to give it time. Wait for the swelling to subside. Rupert's confident it'll only be temporary. You'll be back operating again before you know it'

Finn slammed his glass down on the table. 'Go away, Evie,' he snapped.

Evie jumped but refused to be cowed. He'd been practically yelling at her and telling her to go away for their entire relationship—such as it was. But there'd been other times—tender moments, passionate moments—and that was the real Finn she knew was hidden beneath all his grouchy, arrogant bluster.

She understood why he was pushing her away. Knew that he didn't want to burden her with a man who would be forever less in his eyes because he might not ever again be the one thing that defined him—a surgeon.

But surely that was her choice?

'No. I love you and I'm not going anywhere.'

'I don't want you to love me!' he roared.

Evie came around to his side of the table until she was standing right in front of him. 'Well, you don't always get what you want in life Finn—*not even you*.' She shoved her hands on her hips. 'If you want me to leave then you're going to have to get your butt off that lounge and make me.'

'Oh, I see,' he said, his lip curling. 'This *is* a booty call.'

She endured a deliberately insulting look that raked over her body as if she was sitting in a window in Amsterdam.

'What's the matter, Princess Evie, feeling all horny and frisky with nowhere to put it? *Been a while, has it*? You really needn't have dressed for the occasion. Us one-armed guys can't afford to be choosy, or hadn't you heard?'

Evie had just come from lunch with her sisters and as such was dressed in a pencil skirt that came to just above her knee and a satiny blouse that buttoned up the front and fell gently against her breasts. Her hair was loose and fell around her shoulders.

She ignored him. She would not let his deliberate insults deter her from her goal. 'Let me help you, Finn. Please.'

His good hand snaked out and snagged her wrist. He yanked and she toppled forward, her skirt pulling tight around her thighs as she landed straddling his lap, grabbing at his shoulders for stability.

'Is this what you wanted?' he demanded. 'You want to see how I do this with one hand?' He groped a breast. 'Or this?' he persisted, letting his hand slide down to where her skirt had ridden up, pushing his hand up beneath the fabric, gliding it up her thigh, taking the fabric with him until it was rucked up around her hips and her legs were totally exposed, his hand coming to rest on the curve of one cheek.

Evie felt the drag of desire leaden in her belly as she fought against the seductive allure of her erect nipples and the quivering flesh in his palm. The heat in his gaze burnt into her with all the sear factor of a laser.

'You want to help me feel like a man again?' he sneered, his breath fanning her face. 'You want to take a ride on the one thing I have that *is* fully functional? You want to *screw*, Evie?'

Evie steeled herself against his deliberately crude taunts. He was lashing out. But she wasn't going to respond with the venom his remark deserved.

Because that's what he wanted.

'I just want to love you, Finn,' she said quietly, refusing to break eye contact even though she knew he was trying to goad her into it. Her pulse roared in her ears and her breath sounded all husky and raw. 'Let me love you.'

Evie watched as all the fight went out of him. His hand dropped from her bottom and then he looked away. 'I can't even touch you properly, Evie.'

She grabbed his face and forced him to look at her, his stubble almost soft now it was so long—more spiky than prickly. 'You have this,' she said, her thumb running over the contours of his mouth. 'Which, when it isn't being vicious and cruel, can melt me into a puddle.'

She grabbed his left hand with her right hand and brought it up to her breast. 'And this,' she said, her nipple beading instantly. 'Which knows its way around a woman's body as well as the other.'

Evie saw his pupils dilate as he dropped his gaze to look at his hand on her breast. He stroked his thumb across the aching tip and she shut her eyes briefly.

'And,' she said, dragging herself back from

the completely wanton urge to arch her back, 'this.' She tucked her pelvis in snugly against his and rubbed herself against the hard ridge of his arousal.

'And I can do the rest.'

She put her hands between them and her fingers felt for his button and fly and in that instant Finn stopped wrestling his demons. His mouth lunged for hers, latching on and greedily slaking his thirst as his good hand pulled at her blouse then yanked, popping the buttons.

He grunted in satisfaction, his mouth leaving hers, as her hand finally grasped his erection. His grunt became a groan as he blazed a trail down her neck, his whiskers spiky and erotic against the sensitive skin. He yanked her bra cup aside and closed his hot mouth over a nipple that was already peaked to an unbearable tightness.

Evie's eyes practically rolled back into her head and there was no coherent thought as she mindlessly palmed the length of him and cried out at the delicious graze of his teeth against her nipple.

She wasn't aware his hand had dropped, distracted as she was by the combined pleasure of savage suction and long hot swipes as his tongue continually flayed the hardened tip in his mouth. She wasn't aware of him pushing her hand out the way, of him shoving her underwear aside, of him positioning his erection to her entrance, until it nudged against her thick and hard, and then her body recognised it, knew just what to do and took over, accepting the buck and thrust of him, greedily inflaming and agitating, meeting him one for one, adjusting the tilt of her pelvis to hit just the right spot.

It was no gentle coupling. No languid strokes, no soft caresses and murmured endearments, no long, slow build. It was quick and hasty. Just like their first time. Parted clothes. Desperate clawing at fabric, at skin. At backs and thighs and buttocks. Hitting warp speed instantly, feeling the pull and the burn from the first stroke.

Except this time when Finn cried out with his release, his face buried against her chest, he knew it was goodbye. That he had to get away. From Sydney. From the Sydney Harbour Hospital. From Evie.

From this screwed-up dynamic of theirs.

But for now he needed this. So he clutched her body to his and held on, thrusting and thrusting, prolonging the last vestiges of pleasure, finding a physical outlet for the vortex of grief and pain that swirled inside.

Holding on but saying goodbye.

CHAPTER ONE

Five months later

'WHERE IS HE, Evie?' Richard Lockheart demanded of his daughter. 'Prince Khalid bin Aziz wants Finn Kennedy and only Finn Kennedy to do his quadruple bypass and he's going to donate another million dollars to the hospital to show his appreciation. Sydney Harbour Hospital needs him, Evie. Where is he?'

'I don't know,' Evie said staring out of her father's office window at the boats sailing on the sparkling harbour, wishing she was riding out to sea on one and could leave all her troubles behind her.

'Evie!'

She turned at the imperious command in his voice. 'What makes you think that I know where he is?' she snapped at her father.

'I'm not stupid, Evie. Do you think hospital gossip doesn't reach me all the way over here? I know you and he have a…had a… thing. A fling.' He shrugged. 'Whatever you want to call it. I'm assuming you've kept in touch.'

If Evie needed any other proof of how out of touch her father was with her life, or with life in the trenches generally, she'd just found it. If he knew Finn at all he'd know that Finn wasn't the keeping-in-touch type.

In the aftermath of their frenzied passion five months ago she'd hoped there'd been some kind of breakthrough with him but then he'd disappeared.

Overnight. Literally.

Gladys had told her the next day that he'd gone and handed her a note with seven words.

Goodbye Evie. Don't try and find me.

After all they'd been through—he'd reduced their relationship to seven words.

'Evie!' Richard demanded again, at his daughter's continuing silence.

She glared at her father, who was regarding her as if she was two years old and deliberately defying him, instead of a grown woman. A competent, emergency room physician.

'The state of play between Finn and I is none of your damn business.'

'*Au contraire*,' he said, his brows drawing together. 'What happens at this hospital *is* my business.'

Richard Lockheart took the *business* of Sydney Harbour Hospital very seriously. As its major benefactor he worked tirelessly to ensure it remained the state-of-the-art facility it was, carrying on the legacy of his grandfather, who had founded the hospital. Sometimes she thought he loved the place more than he'd ever loved his wife and his three daughters.

Evie sighed, tired of the fight already. She was just so bloody tired these days. 'Look,' she said, reaching for patience, 'I'm not being deliberately recalcitrant. I really don't know where he is.'

She turned back to the view out the window. His brief impersonal note had been the final axe blow. She'd fought the good fight but there were only so many times a girl could take rejection. So she'd made a decision to forget him and she'd navigated through life these past five months by doing just that. By putting one foot in front of the other and trying not to think about him.

Or what he'd left behind.

But there'd only ever been a finite amount of time she could exist in her state of denial and the first flutterings this morning had brought an abrupt end to that. She couldn't deny that she was carrying his baby any longer.

Or that he deserved to know.

She turned back to her father. 'I think I know somebody who might.'

Evie had spent the last three afternoons pacing back and forth outside Marco D'Avello's outpatients rooms, waiting for his last expectant mother to leave, summoning up the nerve to go in and see him then chickening out each time as the door opened to discharge a patient.

Today was no different. It was five o'clock, the waiting area was empty and his door opened and she sprang from the seat she'd not long plonked herself in for the hundredth time in half an hour and headed for the lift.

'Evie?'

His rich, beautifully accented voice stopped her in her tracks. Evie had to admit that Emily, his wife and a midwife at the hospital, was an exceptionally lucky woman to wake up to that voice every morning. Not to mention the whole dark, sexy Italian stallion thing he had going on.

Just waking up with the person you loved sounded pretty good to her.

He walked towards her. 'I have been watching you outside my door for three days now.' His voice was soft. 'Would you like to see me?'

Evie dithered. She wasn't sure what she wanted. She didn't know what an obstetrician could tell her that she didn't already know. And yet here she was.

'Come,' he murmured, cupping his hand under her elbow.

Evie let herself be led. Why couldn't she love someone like Marco? Someone who was gentle and supportive?

And capable of love.

She heard the door click behind her and sat in the chair he shepherded her towards. 'You are pregnant. Yes?' he said as he walked around to his side of the desk.

Evie startled gaze flew to his. 'How did you…?' she looked down at her belly, placing her hand over the bump that was obvious on her spare athletic frame if she was naked but not discernible yet in the baggy scrubs she wore at work.

Marco smiled. 'It's okay, you are not showing. I'm just a little more…perceptive to this sort of thing. I think it goes with the job.'

Evie nodded, her brain buzzing. She looked at him for long moments. 'I'm sorry. I don't know why I'm here.'

He didn't seemed perturbed by her strange statement. She was pregnant. He was an obstetrician. It was where she should be. Where she should have been a lot earlier than now.

He just seemed to accept it and waited for her to talk some more.

'I haven't told anyone. No one knows,' she said, trying to clarify.

'How many weeks?'

'Eighteen.'

Marco frowned. 'And you haven't seen anyone yet?'

'I've been…busy.' Evie felt her defences rise, not that Marco seemed to be judging her. 'It's always crazy in the emergency department and…time gets away…'

She looked down at her hands still cradling her bump because what excuse was there really to have neglected herself, to have not sought proper antenatal care?

She was a doctor, for crying out loud.

'You have been well?'

Evie nodded, dragging her gaze back to Marco. 'Disgustingly. A few weeks of vague nausea in the beginning. Tired. I've been really tired. But that's it.'

She'd expected the worse when she'd first discovered she was pregnant. She'd figured any child of Finn's was bound to be as disagreeable as his father and make her life hell. But it had been a dream pregnancy to date as far as all that went.

Which had only made it easier for her to deny what was really happening to her body.

'We should do some bloods,' Marco said. 'Why don't you hop up on the couch for a moment and I'll have a feel?'

Evie nodded. She made her way to the narrow examination table and lay staring at the ceiling as Marco palpated her uterus then measured the fundal height with a tape measure. 'Measurements seem spot on for eighteen weeks,' he murmured as he reached over and flipped on a small ultrasound machine.

'No,' Evie said, half sitting, pulling down her scrub top. 'I don't want to…I don't want an ultrasound.'

She didn't want to look at the baby. Not yet. She'd made a huge leap forward today, finally admitting the pregnancy to someone else. She wasn't ready for a meet and greet.

And she knew that made her all kinds of screwed up.

'I'm sorry,' she apologised. 'That's probably not the reaction you're used to.' She couldn't explain why she didn't want to see the baby—she just knew she didn't. Not yet.

Marco turned off the machine and looked down at her and Evie could tell he was choosing his words carefully. 'Evie...you have left it too late to...*do* something about the pregnancy.'

Evie struggled to sit up, gratefully taking Marco's proffered hand as she sat cross-legged on the narrow couch. She had thought about termination but as with everything else pregnancy related she'd shoved it determinedly to one side.

She'd spent the past eighteen weeks not thinking about the baby—her body aiding and abetting her denial by being virtually symptom-free.

She looked at Marco. 'I know. I don't want to.'

She stopped. *Where had that come from?*

Termination had been an option and one, as a doctor and a woman, she firmly believed should be available, but suddenly she knew deep down in the same place that she'd known she loved Finn that she loved his baby too. And that nothing would come between them.

He may not have let her in, let her love him,

but there would be no distance between Finn's child and her.

She gave Marco a half-smile. 'I'm sorry. I don't think I really accepted until the baby moved a few days ago that I was actually pregnant. I'm still trying to…process things.'

He smiled back. 'It's okay. How about we listen to the heartbeat instead and get some bloods done as a first step?'

Evie nodded and lay back and in seconds she was listening to the steady whop-whop-whop of a tiny beating heart. Her eyes filled with tears. 'There really is a baby in there.'

Marco smiled at her gently and nodded. 'Your baby.'

Evie shut her eyes. *Finn's baby.*

Finn Kennedy eased his lean frame into the low squatter's chair and looked out over the vista from the shaded serenity of the wide wraparound veranda. He liked it here in this rambling old house perched on a cliff top overlooking the mighty Pacific Ocean. He gazed over acres of deep blue sea to the horizon, the constant white noise of the surf pounding against the rocks far below a wild serenade.

He liked the tranquillity. For too long he'd been keeping himself busy to block out the pain, drinking to block out the pain, screwing around and pushing himself to the limit to block out the pain.

Who knew that stopping everything and standing still worked better than any of that?

His muscles ached but in a good way. The hard physical labour he'd been doing the last five months had built up his lean body, giving definition to the long smooth muscles in his arms and legs. He felt fitter and more clear-headed than he had in a very long time.

He clenched and unclenched his right hand, marvelling in the full range of movement. He formed a pincer with his index finger and thumb and then tapped each finger in turn onto the pad of his thumb, repeating the process over and over. To think he'd despaired of ever getting any use of it back. It was weaker than his left hand for sure but he'd come a long way.

'As good as a bought one.'

Finn looked up at the approaching form of Ethan Carter, with whom he'd served in the Middle East a decade ago. 'I doubt I'll ever be able to open jam jars.'

Ethan shrugged, handing Finn a beer. 'So don't open jam jars.'

Finn snorted at Ethan's typical Zen-like reasoning as he lowered himself into the chair beside Finn's. Ethan, a Black Hawk pilot, had trained as a psychologist after his discharge from the army and *Beach Haven* had been his brainchild. An exclusive retreat for injured soldiers five hundred kilometres north of Sydney where they could rest, recover, rehabilitate and refocus their lives. Only partially government funded, Ethan worked tirelessly to keep up the very generous private funding that had come Beach Haven's way.

Neither of them said anything for a while, just looked out over the ocean and drank their beer.

'It's time, Finn.'

Finn didn't look at Ethan. He didn't even answer him for a long moment. 'I'm not ready,' he said eventually.

Prior to coming to *Beach Haven*, Finn would have thought being away from Sydney Harbour Hospital, from operating, was a fate worse than death. Now he wasn't sure if he ever wanted to return.

Dropping out and becoming a hermit in a beach shack somewhere was immensely appealing. Maybe he'd even take up surfing.

'Your arm is better. You can't hide here for ever.'

He turned to Ethan and glared at him with a trace of the old Finn. 'Why not?'

'Because this isn't who you are. Because you're using this to avoid your issues.'

'So I should go back to facing them in a high-stress environment where people's lives depend on me?'

'You've healed here, Finn. Physically. And mentally you're much more relaxed. You needed that. But you're not opening up emotionally.'

He shrugged and took a slug of his beer. 'I'm a surgeon, we're not emotional types.'

'No, Finn. Being a surgeon is what you do, not who you are. Beyond all those fancy letters after your name you're just a man who could do nothing but sit and cradle his dying brother while all hell was breaking loose around you. You couldn't help him. You couldn't save him. You couldn't stop him from dying. You're damaged in ways that go far beyond the physical.'

Finn flinched as Ethan didn't even try to pull his punches. In five months they hadn't once spoken about what had happened all those years ago. How Ethan had found a wounded Finn, peppered with shrapnel, holding Isaac.

'But I think you find some kind of emotional release in operating. I think that with every person you save, you bring back a little bit of Isaac. And if you're not going to open up about it, if surgery is your therapy of choice, then I think you should get back to it.'

More silence followed broken only by the pounding of surf.

'So you're kicking me out,' Finn said, staring at the horizon.

Ethan shook his head. 'Nope. I'm recommending a course of treatment. You're welcome to stay as long as you like.'

Finn's thoughts churned like the foam that he knew from his daily foray to the beach swirled and surged against the rocks with the sweep and suck of the tide. He knew Ethan was right, just as he'd known that this reprieve from the world couldn't last.

But his thoughts were interrupted by the crunching of tyres on the gravel drive and the arrival of a little red Mini sweeping into the parking area.

'Are we expecting an arrival today?' Ethan frowned.

'Not as far as I know,' Finn murmured.

They watched as the door opened and a woman climbed out. 'Oh, crap,' Finn said.

* * *

Ten minutes later Evie leaned against the veranda railing, looking out over the ocean view, the afternoon breeze blowing her loose hair off her shoulders. It ruffled the frayed edges of her denim cut-offs and blew the cream cotton of her loose, round-necked peasant blouse against her skin. She breathed the salt tang deep into her lungs.

'Wow,' she said, expelling her breath. 'This is a spectacular view.'

'It's all right,' Finn said, irked that he was enjoying the view of her perky denim-clad backside a hell of a lot more than the magnificent one-hundred-and-eighty-degree ocean view.

Since he'd slunk away in the night after their explosive session on his couch he'd thought about Evie a lot. Probably too much. Some of it R-rated. Most of it involving her big hazel eyes looking at him with love and compassion and pleading with him to let her in.

Up here he'd managed to pigeonhole her and the relationship she'd wanted so desperately as a bad idea. Standing a metre away from her, the long, toned lines of her achingly familiar, he had to clench his fists to stop from reaching for her.

Once upon a time he would have dismissed the impulse as a purely sexual urge. Something he would have felt for any woman standing here after five months of abstinence. A male thing. But solitude and time to think had stripped away his old defence mechanisms and as such he was forced to recognise the truth.

Evie was under his skin.

And it scared the hell out of him. Because she wouldn't be happy with half of him. She would want all of him. And as Ethan had not long ago pointed out, he was damaged.

And it went far beyond that awful day ten years ago.

He didn't know how to love a woman. He doubted he'd ever known. Not even Lydia.

'How did you find me?'

Evie turned to face him, amazed at this version of Finn before her, lounging in a chair, casually knocking back a beer.

Had he ever been this chilled?

Okay, there had been a wariness in his gaze since she'd arrived but this Finn was still a stark contrast to Sydney Harbour Hospital Finn. The old Finn was a serious, driven, sombre professional who oozed energy and drive from every pore. His mind was sharp, his tongue even more so, and his pace had always been frenetic.

His drink of choice was seriously good Scotch.

This Finn was so laid back he may as well have been wearing a Hawaiian shirt and a flower behind his ear. His body was more honed, spare, and his skin had been kissed to a golden honey hue. A far cry from the haggard shadow he'd been when last she'd seen him.

Had he been surfing all this time?

The incredible blue of his eyes, so often frigid with disapproval, were like warm tropical waters amidst the golden planes of his stubbly face. And she wanted to dive in.

She'd been nervous that he'd take one look at her and know she was pregnant. Which was ridiculous given that it would be at least another month, maybe more, before it was obvious to anyone. But she really needn't have worried. This Finn didn't look like he'd be bothered if she'd turned up with his triplets.

Something rose in her chest, dark and ugly. It twisted and burned and she realised she was jealous. This was the kind of Finn she'd longed for, had known was there somewhere. The one he'd never shown her.

'Daddy get a private detective?' he goaded.

His voice had an edge that she recognised as the old Finn and she found herself responding accordingly. She was like Pavlov's dog, still salivating over the slightest crumb.

She cleared her throat as emotion lodged like a fist in her trachea. 'Lydia.'

'Lydia?' Finn sat up. '*Lydia* told you I was here?' Isaac's widow, the woman he'd had a seriously screwed-up co-dependent relationship with in the aftermath of his brother's death, had been talking to Evie?

He frowned. '*You know Lydia?*'

Evie nodded calmly. Well, she'd met her anyway—she still had no clue as to their relationship. 'I met her outside your apartment a couple of days after you left. She came to pick up some stuff for you. Told me you were okay. That you needed space. Time… She gave me her card.'

Finn shut his eyes and leaned back into the canvas hammock of the squatter's chair. Trust Lydia to interfere. He opened his eyes to find her looking at him.

'Your arm is better, I see.'

Finn looked down at it. He clenched and unclenched his fingers automatically, still amazed that he could do so. 'Yes.'

Evie pressed her butt hard into the railing. She wanted to launch herself at him, throw herself into his lap, hug him to her, tell him she'd known it would get better, that he'd just needed a little faith and a lot of patience. But he didn't look so laid back now and memories of what had happened last time she had been in his lap overrode everything else.

There was even more between them now than there'd ever been—more than he certainly knew—and she couldn't think about any of it until she had him back in Sydney, until after he'd operated on their celebrity patient, until after she'd told him about the baby...

'You must be very relieved,' Evie murmured.

Finn didn't want to make small talk with her. His mind had been clear ten minutes ago and now it was all clouded up again.

Seeing Evie after five months' break made him realise how much he'd missed her wide hazel eyes and her interesting face. How much he'd taken her presence for granted when they'd worked in the same hospital, when she'd been there for him during his ops. How much he'd come to depend on seeing her, even though he'd pushed her away at every turn.

He'd been able to ignore all of that five hundred kilometres away from her—out of sight out of mind. But it was impossible to ignore now. She made him want things he didn't know how to articulate.

And he wanted her gone.

So he could go back to ignoring her and all the stuff that bubbled to the surface whenever she was around all over again.

'Why are you here?' he demanded.

Evie swallowed at his sullen enquiry. His gaze was becoming chilly again and she shivered. 'Prince Khalid bin Aziz.'

Finn frowned at the name from his past. Several years ago he'd revived a man who had collapsed in front of him on the street a couple of blocks from the hospital. He'd had no way of knowing at the time that the man was a Saudi oil prince. There'd been no robes, no staff, no security. He'd just been another heart to start and Finn's medical training had taken over.

But it had certainly worked out well for the hospital, which had benefited from a huge donation.

'What does he want?'

'He wants you.' *Not as badly as she did, however.* 'He needs a quadruple bypass and he wants you *and only you* to perform it.'

Finn gripped his beer bottle harder as Evie opened a door he'd shut firmly behind him and a surge of adrenaline hit him like a bolt from the blue. He could almost smell the chemical cleanliness of the operating room, hear the dull slap as an instrument hit his gloved hand, feel the heat of the overhead lights on the back of his neck.

He shook his head, quashing the powerful surge of anticipation. 'I'm not ready to come back.'

Evie's looked down at him as he absently clenched and unclenched his right hand. Her heart banged loudly in her chest. *What on earth was he talking about?* Finn was a surgeon. The best cardiothoracic surgeon there was. He had to come back. And not just for the amir.

For him. For his sanity. For his dignity. The Finn she knew *needed* to work.

'You look physically capable,' she said, keeping her voice neutral.

Finn pushed up out of the chair as the decision he'd been circling around for five months crystallised. He walked to the railing, keeping a distance between them, his gaze locking on the horizon. 'I don't know if I'm going to come back.'

Evie stared at his profile. 'To the Harbour?'

Finn shook his head as he tested the words out loud. 'To surgery.'

Evie blinked, her brain temporarily shutting down at the enormity of his admission. Quit being a surgeon?

That was sacrilege.

She turned around slowly so she too was facing the horizon. Her hand gripped the railing as the line between the earth and the sky seemed to tilt. 'My father will not be pleased,' she joked, attempting to lighten the moment while her thoughts and emotions jumbled themselves into an almighty tangle.

'Ah, yes, how is the great Richard Lockheart?'

Evie would have to have been deaf not to hear the contempt in Finn's voice. It was fair to say that Finn was not on Team Richard. But, then, neither was she.

'Already counting the pennies from the big fat donation Prince Khalid has promised the hospital.'

Evie wondered if Finn remembered that it was through Prince Khalid's misfortune that she'd first met him. At the gala dinner that the prince had thrown in Finn's honour the first time he'd donated one million dollars to the Sydney Harbour Hospital's cardiothoracic department.

Finn had been as unimpressed as she to be there.

He snorted. 'Of course. I should have known there would be money involved.'

Evie had never heard such coldness in Finn's voice before. Not where his work was concerned, and it frightened her. She was used to it regarding her and anything of a remotely personal nature. But not his job.

She'd never thought she'd have to convince him to come back to work. She'd just assumed he'd jump back in as soon as he possibly could.

Just how long had his hand been recovered for?

'So don't do it for him,' she said battling to keep the rise of desperation out of her voice. 'Or for the money. Do it for the prince.'

'There are any number of very good cardiac surgeons in Sydney.'

'He doesn't want very good. He wants the best.'

Finn turned to face her, propping his hip against the railing. 'No.'

Evie turned too, at a complete loss as she faced him. 'Please.'

She seemed to always be asking him for something he wasn't prepared to give. Saying, *please, Finn, please*. And she was heartily sick of it. And sick of being rejected.

And if she wasn't carrying his baby she'd

just walk right away. But she was. And he needed to know—whatever the fallout might be.

She opened her mouth to tell him. Not to bribe him into doing what she wanted but because she could see his mind was made up, and before he sent her away for the last time, he had to know.

But Ethan striding out onto the veranda interrupted them. 'Finn—' Finn looked over Evie's shoulder. 'Oh…sorry…I thought I heard the car leave,' Ethan said, smiling apologetically at Evie as he approached.

'It's fine,' Evie murmured.

'What's up?' Finn asked, dragging his gaze away from Evie's suddenly pale face.

'What's the name of that agency you were telling me about?'

Finn frowned. 'The medical staffing one? Why?'

'Hamish's father-in-law had a heart attack and died two hours ago. He's taking two weeks off. I've been ringing around everywhere but no one's available and I can't run this place without a medico on board, it's a government regulation.'

'For God's sake, Ethan,' Finn said, his voice laced with exasperation, having had this conversation too many times before. '*I'm* a doctor.'

Ethan shook his head firmly. 'You're a client.'

Finn shoved his hand on his hip. 'These are extenuating circumstances.'

Ethan chuckled. 'No dice, buddy. Them's the rules.'

'You never used to be such a stickler for the rules.'

Ethan clapped him on the back. 'I wasn't running my own business back then.'

Evie was surprised at the obvious affection between the two men. Surprised even more at the spurt of jealousy. Finn wasn't the touchy-feely kind. He maintained professional relationships with his colleagues and he'd been known to sit at the bar over the road from the hospital and knock back a few whiskies with them from time to time but he was pretty much a solo figure.

He and Ethan, a big bear of a man with a grizzly beard and kind eyes, seemed to go back a long way.

'Problem?' she asked, at Finn's obvious frustration.

Finn shook his head then stopped as an idea took hold. He raked his gaze over her and knew it would probably be something he would come to regret, but choices were limited in the middle of nowhere.

Maybe the current pain in his butt could be Ethan's silver lining. 'Evie can do it.'

'What?' she gaped, her pulse spiking. 'Do what?'

Ethan smiled at Evie apologetically. 'I'm sorry. He's not very good with social nuances, is he?'

'She's a fully qualified, highly trained, *very good* emergency doctor,' Finn continued, ignoring Ethan's remark.

'You can't just go springing jobs on people like that and acting like they have no choice but to take them,' Ethan chided, his smile getting wider and wider. 'Not cool, man. Maybe you should try asking the lady?'

Finn turned to Evie, his palms finding her upper arms, curling around her biceps. 'I'll come back and do Khalid's surgery. But only if you do the two weeks here first.'

Ethan crossed his arms. 'That's not asking.'

Evie felt her belly plummet as if she'd just jumped out of a plane. She wasn't sure if was due to his snap decision, his compliment over her medical skills or his touch but she couldn't think when he looked at her with need in his eyes.

Even if it was purely professional.

'C'mon, Princess Evie,' Finn murmured, trying to cut through the confusion he could see in her hazel eyes. 'Step outside your comfort zone for a while. Live a little.'

'You suck at asking,' Ethan interjected.

Evie swallowed as she became caught up in the heady rush of being needed by Finn. Not even the nickname grated.

Why not?

It would kill two birds with one stone—Khalid got his op and she bought herself some time. And her father had told her to do *anything* to get Finn back.

'Okay,' she said, hoping her voice didn't sound as shaky as it felt leaving her throat.

Finn nodded and looked at Ethan. 'You've got yourself a doctor.'

Ethan looked from one to the other, his bewildered look priceless. Like he couldn't quite believe that in less than a minute his major problem had been settled.

Neither, frankly, could Evie.

CHAPTER TWO

EVIE CLIMBED ONTO the back of the four-wheeler behind Ethan the next morning for the grand tour. *Beach Haven* retreat covered a couple of hundred acres and wasn't something that could be quickly traversed on foot. Finn, who had disappeared shortly after he'd bribed her into staying for two weeks, was still nowhere to be seen. She didn't ask Ethan where he was and he didn't tell her.

Her father hadn't been happy with the two-week delay but as the prince's blocked arteries had been found on a routine physical and hadn't been symptomatic, the surgery wasn't urgent.

Their first port of call was the clinic. It could be seen from the homestead and she'd be able to walk easily to and from along the track, but as it was just the first stop of many today Ethan drove them across.

It looked like an old worker's cottage from

the outside but had been renovated entirely on the inside with a waiting area, a couple of rooms with examination tables and a minor ops room. A small dispensary with common medications, a storeroom, a toilet and a kitchenette completed the well-equipped facility. Thought had also been given to disabled access with the addition of ramps, widened doors and handrails.

'Clinic starts at ten every morning. First come first served. There's rarely a stampede. They usually come to see me.'

Evie cocked an eyebrow. 'For therapy?' He nodded. 'I wouldn't have thought you'd have any takers.'

Ethan shrugged. 'It's a pre-req for a place here. Weekly therapy—whether they like it or not.'

She thought not liking it would be the predominant feeling amongst a bunch of battle-weary soldiers. 'Does that include Finn?'

He nodded. 'No exceptions.'

Evie absorbed the information. Maybe that was why he seemed so chilled? But... surely not. The Finn she knew wasn't capable of talking about his issues. 'I don't imagine those sessions would be very enlightening.'

Ethan laughed. 'He's pretty guarded, that's for sure. But...' he shrugged '...you can lead a horse to water... I can't force him or any-one else to open up. I just hope like hell they do. In my opinion, there's not a man who's seen active duty who couldn't do with some therapy.'

'Is that why you opened this place?' Evie asked. 'A ruse to get soldiers into therapy?'

He laughed again and Evie found her-self wondering why it was she couldn't fall for someone like Ethan. He was attractive enough in a shaggy kind of a way with a ready smile and an easy manner.

'Kind of,' he said, his voice big and gruff like the rest of him. 'Returned soldiers have issues. Those who have been physically in-jured even more so. It's too easy for them to slip through the cracks. Succumb to feel-ings of uselessness, hopelessness and despair. Here they're able to continue their rehab, con-tribute to society and find a little perspective.'

'And you're the perspective?' she asked, smiling.

Ethan looked embarrassed but smiled back. 'Anyway...' he said, looking around, 'clinic is done by twelve and then your day is your own as long as you stay on the property and have your pager on you in case an emergency arises.'

'Does that happen very often?'

Ethan shook his head. 'The last one was a couple of months ago when there was an incident with a nail gun.'

She raised an eyebrow. 'Do I want to know?'

He grinned and shook his head. 'Nope.'

Evie nodded slowly, also looking around. 'So, that's it? A two-hour clinic and the odd nail-gun emergency?'

Ethan nodded. 'Think you can cope?' he teased.

Compared to the frenetic pace of a busy city emergency department Evie felt as if Ethan had just handed her the keys to paradise. And there was a beach to boot! 'I think I can hack the pace,' she murmured. 'In fact, I think I may just have died and gone to heaven.'

He grinned. 'C'mon, I'll show you the rest.'

Ten minutes later they pulled up at what appeared to be a massive shed that actually housed an Olympic-sized indoor swimming pool and a large gym area where she caught up with Bob, the physiotherapist she'd met last night. He was in the middle of a session with two below-knee amputees so they didn't chat.

From there it was another ten minutes to a series of three smaller sheds. The side doors were all open and the sounds of electric saws and nail guns pierced the air as Ethan cut the bike engine.

'This is where we build the roof trusses I was telling you about last night,' Ethan said as they dismounted.

With a noticeably absent Finn over dinner last night, Ethan had filled her in on the flood-recovery project the retreat participants contributed to during their stay. Several extreme weather events had led to unprecedented flooding throughout Australia over the previous two years and demand for new housing was at a premium. Roof trusses were part of that. It was a small-scale project perfect for Ethan's ragtag band of clients, which aided both the flood and the soldiers' recovery.

It was win-win.

They entered the nearest workshop, which was a hive of activity. The aroma of cut timber immediately assailed Evie and she pulled it deep into her lungs. One by one the men stopped working.

'I suspect,' Ethan whispered out of the side of his mouth, 'you may well see an increase in visits to the clinic in the next few days. Just to check you out. Not a lot of women around here.'

Evie smiled as all but one lone nail gun pistoned away obliviously. It stopped too after a few moments and the owner turned and looked at her.

It was Finn.

Evie's breath caught in her throat. He was wearing faded jeans and an even more faded T-shirt that clung in all the good places. A tool belt was slung low on his hips. Used to seeing him in baggy scrubs, her brain grappled with the conflicting images.

Her body however, now well into the second trimester and at the mercy of a heightened sex drive, responded on a completely primitive level.

Tool-Man Finn was hot.

A wolf whistle came from somewhere in the back.

'Okay, okay back to work.' Ethan grinned. 'Don't scare our doctor away before her first day.'

One by one they resumed their work. Except Finn, who downed his nail gun, his arctic gaze firmly fixed on her as he strode in her direction.

'Uh-oh,' Ethan said out of the corner of his mouth. 'He doesn't look too happy.'

Evie couldn't agree more. She should be apprehensive. But he looked pretty damn sexy, coming at her with all that coiled tension. Like he might just slam her against the nearest wall and take her, like he had their first time.

'I don't think happy is in his vocabulary.'

Finn pulled up in front of Ethan—who seriously should know better than to bring a woman into an environment where most of the men hadn't seen one in weeks—and glared at his friend. *Who had clearly gone mad.*

'What is *she* doing here?' he demanded.

Ethan held up his hands. 'Just showing the lady around.'

'She only needs to know where the clinic is,' Finn pointed out.

'Well, apart from common courtesy,' Ethan murmured, his voice firm, '*Evie* really should know the lie of the land in case of an emergency.'

Finn scowled at his friend's logic. 'Now she knows.' He turned and looked at Evie in her clothes from yesterday, her hair loose. 'This is no place for a woman,' he ground out.

Having been in the army for a decade and here for almost five months, Finn knew these men and men just like them. Even hiding away, licking their wounds, sex was always on their mind.

Evie felt her hackles rise. Had she slipped

back into the Fifties? She glared at him, her gaze unwavering. 'You ought to talk,' she snapped, pleased the background noise kept their conversation from being overheard. 'What kind of a place is this for a surgeon, Finn? Wielding a nail gun when you should be wielding a scalpel!'

Finn ignored the dig. 'Get her out of here,' he said to Ethan.

Finn scowled again as Ethan grinned but breathed a sigh of relief when Evie followed Ethan out, every pair of eyes in the workshop glued to her butt.

His included.

On their next leg, they passed a helipad and a small hangar with a gleaming blue and white chopper sitting idle.

'Yours?' she asked.

He nodded. 'Handy piece of transport in the middle of nowhere.'

They drove to a large dam area, which had been the source of the silver perch they'd eaten last night. Above it evenly spaced on a grassy hill sat ten pre-fab dongas.

'Each one has four bedrooms, a bathroom, a kitchen and common area,' Ethan explained, as he pulled up under a shady stand of gumtrees near the dam edge and cut the engine.

'They're not luxurious but they're better than anything any of us slept in overseas.'

'So your capacity is forty?'

'Actually, it's forty-five if you count the homestead accommodation,' Ethan said, dismounting and walking over to inspect the water. 'That's over and above you, me, Bob and Finn.'

Evie nodded, also walking over to the water's edge. The sun was warm on her skin and she raised her face to it for long moments. She could hear the low buzz of insects and the distant whine of a saw.

Ethan waited for a while and said, 'So… you and Finn…'

Evie opened her eyes and looked at him. 'What about me and Finn?'

'You're…colleagues? Friends…?'

Evie considered Ethan's question for a while. She didn't know how to define them with just one word. Colleagues, yes. Lovers, yes. Soon to be parents, yes. But friends…?

She shrugged. 'It's…complicated.'

Ethan nodded. 'He's a complicated guy.'

Evie snorted at the understatement of the century. 'You've known him for a while?'

Ethan picked up a stone at his feet and skipped it across the surface. 'We served together overseas.'

'You know his brother died over there?'

'I know.'

'It's really messed with his head,' she murmured.

Ethan picked up another stone and looked at it. 'You love him?' he asked gently.

Evie swallowed as Ethan followed his direct question with a direct look. She thought about denying it, but after five months of denying it it felt good to say it to someone. 'Yes.' She gave a self-deprecating laugh. 'He's not exactly easy to love, though, you know? And God knows I've tried not to…'

Evie paused. She had a feeling that Ethan knew exactly how hard Finn was to love. 'I think what happened with his brother really shut him down emotionally,' she murmured.

She knew she was making another excuse for him but she couldn't even begin to imagine how awful it would be to hold Bella or Lexi in her arms as they died. The thought of losing her sisters at all was horrifying. But like that?

How did somebody stay normal after that?

How did it not push a person over the edge?

Ethan looked back at the stone in his hand, feeling its weight and its warmth before letting it fly to skim across the surface. 'Yes, it did. But I think Finn had issues that predated the tragedy with Isaac,' he said carefully.

Evie snapped to attention. 'He told you that?'

Ethan snorted. 'No. This *is* Finn, remember. He's always been pretty much a closed book, Evie. At least as long as I've known him. And we go back a couple of years before what happened with Isaac. He's been much, much worse since then but he wasn't exactly the life of the party before that. Part of it is the things he'd seen, the injuries, the total…mayhem that is war. A person shuts themselves down to protect themselves from that kind of carnage. But I think there's even more than that with Finn, stuff from his distant past.'

Evie stilled as the enormity of what she faced hit home. If Ethan was right she was dealing with something bigger than his grief. She looked at Ethan helplessly, her hand seeking the precious life that grew inside her, needing to anchor herself in an uncertain sea. 'I don't know how to reach him through all that.'

Ethan shrugged. 'I don't know how you do it either but I do know that he's crying out for help and after that little performance in the workshop, I think you're the one woman

who can do it. I have never seen Finn so…
emotionally reactive as just now.'

Evie cocked an eyebrow. 'Is that what you
call it?'

He grinned. 'Don't give up on him, Evie.
I think you'll make a human being out of
him yet.'

Ethan had been right—word had got out.
Evie's clinic was bustling that first morning
with the most pathetic ailments she'd ever
treated. But it felt good to be able to prac-
tise medicine where there was no pressure
or stress or life-and-death situations and the
men were flirty and charming and took the
news of her pretend boyfriend waiting back
home for her good-naturedly.

She and Bob had lunch together on the
magnificent homestead veranda serenaded
by the crash of the surf. She yawned as Bob
regaled her with the details of the nail-gun
incident.

'Sorry,' she apologised with a rueful smile.
'It must be the sea air.'

Bob took it in his stride. 'No worries. You
should lie down and have a bit of a kip, love.
A siesta. Reckon the Italians have that right.'

Evie was awfully tempted. The pregnancy
had made her tired to the bone and by the

time she arrived home after manic twelve-hour shifts at Sydney Harbour she was utterly exhausted. She already felt like she was in a major sleep deficit—and the baby wasn't even out yet! She fantasised every day about midday naps and she could barely drag herself out of bed on her days off.

But it didn't seem right to wander off for a nanny nap in broad daylight—was that even allowed?

'Go on,' Bob insisted as she yawned again. 'There's nothing for you to do here and you have your pager.'

Evie hesitated for a moment longer then thought, What the hell?

She pulled the suitcase off her bed—it must have been delivered while she'd been working that morning. She'd tasked Bella with the job of packing two weeks' worth of clothes for her because, as a fashion designer, Evie knew her sister would choose with care. Her youngest sister Lexi, on the other hand, who was thirty-two weeks pregnant and time poor, would have just shoved in the first things that came to hand.

As her head hit the pillow her thoughts turned to Finn, as they always did. Should she tell him, shouldn't she tell him? When to tell him? Here? Back in Sydney? When would be a good time?

But the lack of answers was even more wearying than the questions and within a minute the sound of the ocean and the pull of exhaustion had sucked her into a deep, deep sleep.

Evie woke with a start three hours later. She looked at the clock. She'd slept for three freaking hours?

She must have been more tired than she'd thought!

She certainly hadn't felt this rested in a long time. Maybe after two weeks here she'd have caught up on the sleep she needed.

She stretched and stared at the ceiling for a moment or two, her hand finding her belly without conscious thought.

'Well, baby,' she said out loud. 'Should I track your father down and tell him right now or should I wait till we're back in Sydney and he's done the op?'

Evie realised she should feel silly, talking to a tiny human being in utero who couldn't respond, but she'd spent so much time avoiding anything to do with the life inside her that it suddenly seemed like the most natural thing in the world—talking to her baby.

'Move now if you think I should tell him today.'

Again, quite silly. If she was going to rely on airy-fairy reasoning to inform her critical decisions, it'd probably make more sense to flip a coin.

But then the baby moved. And not some gentle fluttering, is-it-or-isn't it, maybe-it's-just-wind kind of movement. It was a kick. A very definite kick. As if the baby was shaping up to play soccer for Australia.

Crap. The baby had spoken.

Twenty minutes later she'd changed into a loose, flowing sundress that she'd never seen before but which fitted her perfectly. Bella had attached a note to say, 'Designed this especially for you. xxx.'

It was floaty and feminine with shoestring straps—perfect for the beach and the warm September day. And exactly what she needed to face Finn.

Finn couldn't be found around the homestead but Ethan came out as she was standing at the veranda railing, contemplating the horizon.

'Good clinic this morning,' he said.

Evie smiled. 'I've never known a bunch of tough guys see a doctor for such trifling complaints.' Ethan laughed and she joined him. 'I don't suppose you know where Finn might be?' she asked, when their laughter petered out.

'I'd try the beach.' He inclined his head towards the well-worn track that lead to the safety-railed cliff edge and the two hundred and twenty stairs that delivered the intrepid traveller straight onto the beach.

They were not for the faint-hearted…

'He normally swims everyday around this time.'

'Am I allowed to go that far away?' she asked.

Ethan laughed. 'Of course. It's not that far. And even though it isn't a private beach, we kind of consider it as within the property boundaries.'

She smiled. 'Thanks.'

Halfway down she stood aside to let a buff-looking guy in boardies and a backpack run past, his below-knee prosthesis not seeming to hinder him an iota. He nodded at her as he pounded upwards and she turned to watch him as he scaled the stairs as if they were nothing.

Her gaze drifted all the way up the sheer

cliff face to the very top. She was dreading *walking* back—running just seemed insane.

Her foot hit the warm sand a few minutes later and her gaze scanned the wide arc of yellow, unpatrolled beach for Finn. She couldn't see him but as she walked closer to the thundering ocean she could see a towel discarded on the sand and she looked out at the water, trying to see a head amongst the continually rolling breakers.

Her heart beat in sync with the ocean as she searched in vain through the wild pounding surf and a hundred disaster scenarios scuttled through her head. She calmed herself with the knowledge that he was a strong swimmer and ignored the ominous power of the surging ocean. Then she spotted his head popping up out of the water. He was quite a distance out but she could see his wet hair was sleek, like a seal's pelt, and his shoulders were broad and bare.

She sat on the sand next to his towel and waited.

Finn was aware of Evie from the minute she'd set foot on the beach. Some sixth sense had alerted him and he'd watched her advance towards the shoreline, obviously looking for him.

And, of course, she looked utterly gorgeous in a dress that blew across her body, outlining her athletic legs, her hair whipping across her face, the shoestring straps baring lovely collar bones and beautiful shoulders.

Just looking at her made him hard and he was grateful for the cover of ocean.

It had been so long since he'd touched her. He wanted to stride up the beach, push her back into the sand and bury himself in her. But he hated the feelings she roused in him and the loss of control he exhibited when he was with her.

Besides…it would just put them back at square one when he'd tried so hard—and succeeded—at putting distance between them.

He could tell, though, even from this distance, she was here to chat. And, God knew, he didn't want to chat with her. Right now the only thing he wanted to do with her involved being naked and he was going to stay right here until he'd worn the impulse down.

He swam against and with the strong current until he was chilled to the bone and his arm ached. A part of him hoped she'd get sick of waiting and just leave. Or maybe her pager would go off. But she sat stubbornly staring out to sea, watching him until finally the chill was unbearable and, admitting defeat, he strode from the surf.

She handed him his towel as he drew level with her and he took it wordlessly, rubbing vigorously at his body. When he was done he wrapped it around his waist and threw himself down next to her, taking care to leave a gap. She didn't say anything to him as they both sat and watched the ocean for a while, the sun's rays beginning to work their magic on the ice that seemed to penetrate right down to his bones.

Although the ice around his heart was as impenetrable as always.

'I hear you have a boyfriend,' he said after a while.

Evie, her brain still grappling with the perfect words to tell Finn he was going to be a father and her stupid pregnant hormones still all aflutter from his sexy Adonis-rising-from-the-ocean display, didn't register the terseness in his tone.

'A cosmetic surgeon who owns a Porsche and comes from North Shore money,' he continued.

Evie bit back a smile at the ill-disguised contempt in his voice. When choosing her fake boyfriend she'd deliberately chosen all the attributes Finn would despise. 'Well, I figured if I was going to have a make-believe boyfriend I might as well go all out.'

Finn wasn't mollified. 'He sounds like a tosser.'

Evie smiled at the ocean. 'Because he does lips and boobs or because of the Porsche?'

Finn glared at her as she continued to stare at the horizon. 'Is that what you want, Princess Evie? Some blue-blooded prince to keep up your royal lineage?'

She turned to look at him, her nostrils flaring as the scent of sea salt and something her hormones recognised as quintessentially Finn enveloped her. 'I think you know who I want.'

And suddenly the roar of the ocean faded as the pounding of her pulse took over. The fact she was supposed to be telling him about their baby also faded as her heart drummed a primitive beat perfectly at home in this deserted windswept landscape. The world of the beach shrank until there was just him and her and the sun stroking warm fingers over their skin, lulling her common sense into a stupor. His bare chest and shoulders teased her peripheral vision, his sexy stubble and wet, ruffled hair taunted her front and centre.

'I've only ever wanted you, Finn,' she murmured, her breath rough as her gaze fell to his mouth. Wanting to feel it on hers. To feel it everywhere. 'And right now all I can think about is how good we are together.'

Finn shut his eyes, images of how good they were rolling through his brain as seductively as her voice, like a siren from the sea. He opened them again and her hazel eyes were practically silver with desire. 'Evie...'

Her breasts grew heavy at the rawness of his voice. Longing snaked through her belly, hot and hard and hungry as she lifted her hand to his face, ran her fingers over his mouth. 'I've wanted to kiss you every day for five months,' she murmured.

Finn gently grabbed her wrist, intent on setting her away, but the breeze blew the scent of her shampoo, of her skin right into his face, enveloping him in a cloud of memories, and he knew he wasn't strong enough. Not after five months of denial.

'Oh, hell,' he half muttered, half groaned as he slid his hand from her wrist into her hair, pulling her head close and lowering his mouth to hers.

He'd lain awake at night thinking about her kiss. And it was as good as he remembered. Better. She opened to him on a sigh, moved into the shelter of his arms as if she belonged there and he felt the last of the cold disappear from his bones as an intense heat roared and raged through his marrow.

And then he was hot everywhere.

Their tongues tangoed as he pressed her back onto the sand, his thigh instantly pushing between hers, his hand automatically stroking down her neck, across her shoulders before claiming a breast, firmer and rounder even than he remembered, the nipple beading instantly beneath his palm.

Evie moaned as she arched her back, pushing herself into his hand more, the ache of the aroused tip mirroring the ache between her legs. She rubbed against his thigh to relieve it but he only pushed harder against her, stoking the need higher.

And then with a muffled curse against her mouth he was over her, on top of her, and she revelled in the pressure of him pushing her into the warm sand, the imprint of each grain against the backs of her calves, the feel of the naked planes of his back dry and warm from the sun beneath her hands.

Her head spun from his kiss, her breath was short and choppy and her belly dipped and tightened with every thrust and parry of his tongue. And if it hadn't been for a lone seagull landing practically on top of them and startling them both out of their stupor, Evie had no doubt they would have gone all the way, oblivious to everything but the primitive imperative of their bodies.

Evie broke off their kiss as sense invaded their bubble and she became aware they were making out on a beach and anyone with two eyes and a pair of binoculars could be watching them from the cliff top. Not to mention anyone coming down the stairs from the retreat copping an eyeful.

Finn uttered another curse and rolled off her, flopping onto his back, his chest heaving, his pulse battering his temples, his erection throbbing painfully.

'Finn.' She reached for his arm but he vaulted upright abruptly and she knew he was already regretting what had happened.

'I'm sorry,' he said. 'That shouldn't have happened.'

Evie sighed as she too sat, her body still zinging from their kisses. 'Why not?' she asked. 'We're both adults, Finn.'

Finn shook his head vehemently. 'We're not going down this road again, Evie,' he said.

Evie smoothed her dress over her knees. *Tell him.* Tell him they were on the road together whether he liked it or not. 'Would it be so bad?'

'I lose my head when I'm around you and I don't like it.'

'That's a shame,' she said, trying to lighten the moment. *Tell him!* 'I like it when you lose your head.'

'Damn it, Evie,' he barked, looking at her, her lips full and soft from his ravaging. 'I don't. I don't like it. I almost had you naked on your back on this beach.'

She placed her hand on his forearm. It felt warm and solid in her palm and she never wanted to let go.

Tell him!

But she couldn't. She didn't want to use the baby to win him. 'Finn…I've known you for five years and I've never seen you so relaxed. So why don't you just…relax and see where this takes us?'

Finn shrugged her hand away. 'You want more than I'm prepared to give. And you deserve it, too.' He stood and looked down at her. 'We've got two weeks here together. Let's just stay away from each other, okay?'

He didn't give her a chance to reply as he turned on his heel. The baby thumped around inside her as she watched him stride off. No doubt it was trying to make her feel guilty for not accomplishing what she'd come to the beach to achieve.

'Sorry, baby,' she whispered. 'Not going to happen. I'll tell him when we get to Sydney—promise.'

CHAPTER THREE

AND STAY AWAY from each other they did. At least, Finn steered clear of her anyway.

Painstakingly...

His distance reminded her of how they had co-existed for years at the hospital. Aware of each other, of what might have happened that first night they'd met at the gala in Finn's honour had her father not come along and given her away as a Lockheart. Aware of something bubbling beneath the surface but neither crossing the professional divide—junior doctor and consultant.

Even her catastrophic relationship with Stuart now seemed a desperate attempt to cling to someone she could have, to distract herself from someone she couldn't.

But despite all that, their mutual attraction—subversive, unspoken—had simmered away until it had flared out of control one day and little by little she'd wedged herself into his life. He hadn't liked it, he didn't like it now, but it was simply too big to ignore.

Although she had to give it to Finn, the man did denial better than anyone she knew.

So Evie did what she had been raised to do from an early age by a father who'd prized her social skills above her brains and talent—she fitted in.

Schmoozed.

She got to know the gang. Mingled with the guys as they went about their day-to-day business—despite Finn's scowls. Took quad lessons with whoever was around to teach her. Helped Tom out at the gym and in the hydrotherapy pool. Became a sounding board for Ethan over a couple of the guys he was worried about.

And she slept in and read a book a day from the extensive library at the homestead and ate the delicious food cooked by Reginald, an ex-army chef, and soaked in the sea air and the sunshine like a giant sponge. She felt good—fit and healthy—and knew from the mirror that the tired smudges beneath her eyes had disappeared and that her skin was glowing and her hair shone.

She'd also taken to swimming after her clinic each day. She tagged along with a group of the guys and lolled in ankle-deep waters as they ran drills on the beach. Despite being a strong swimmer, she was never quite game enough to go out too far, preferring the gentler push and pull of the shallows. Such a desolate windswept section of the coastline, dominated by sheer cliffs and rocky outcrops, needed to be respected.

After a couple of hours of swimming and soaking up the sun they'd head back again. Oftentimes Finn would be on his way down. The men would greet him enthusiastically and if any of them thought Finn's reserved response was odd they never commented. They seemed to respect him and his personal space and if it made Evie sad to think that Finn came to the beach alone when he could have had company, she was obviously the only one.

Two weeks flew by so fast and Evie couldn't believe it was her last day as she dressed for her final sojourn to the beach. Thoughts of how relaxing it had been here filled her head as she rounded the side of the veranda and literally ran smack bang into Finn.

'Sorry,' she apologised as he grabbed her to steady her from their impact.

For the briefest moment their bodies were pressed together and neither of them moved as heat arced between them. Then Finn set her back and stepped away.

'Going down for your daily flirt, I see?' he said through stiff lips.

He looked her up and down as if she was wearing a skimpy bikini instead of a very sensible pair of boardies and the un-sexiest sun shirt ever made. Apart from the fact the shirt was tight around her bust due to the pregnancy, everywhere else pretty much hung and Evie was grateful for the extra layers of fabric as her bump seemed to become more and more noticeable to her by the day.

She decided to ignore the jibe. 'Have you packed up all your stuff for the trip home tomorrow?'

Her time in paradise was over—Hamish would be back tonight and she and Finn would return to Sydney tomorrow. A flutter wormed its way through her belly at the thought of going back. Part of her wanted to stay—hole up here and forget the world. With the pound of the ocean below, it was incredibly tempting. But she was a fighter, not a hider. And real life beckoned.

The thought of being in a car with Finn for five hours, of having him back in Sydney, of telling him what she knew she must, made her pulse trip.

But it had to be done.

'Nothing to pack—I still have my apartment with everything I'll need,' he said. 'And I'll be coming straight back here after Khalid's discharge.'

Evie blinked. 'You're coming back?'

Finn gave a curt nod. 'Yes. I'm done with surgery.' He hadn't been sure when she'd first arrived but two weeks back in her company had crystallised his decision.

Evie stared at him blankly for a moment then allowed the bubble of laughter rising in her throat an escape. He seriously thought he could just waltz in and do a one-off and not be sucked back into a world he'd thrived in?

Even she knew being a surgeon was like oxygen to him.

'You know as well as I do that you'll change your mind the minute you step foot in your old operating theatre.'

Finn hated how her laughter trivialised something he'd grappled with for a long time.

And that that she knew him so well.

It had been hell having her around the last two weeks. Hearing her voice and catching glimpses of her everywhere. Reminding him of them. Of his old life. Watching the guys flirt with her and then talk about her—*Evie this and Evie that.* The calm that he'd found here over the last months had well and truly evaporated and he desperately wanted it back.

The sooner he fulfilled his end of the bargain, the sooner he could find it again.

But he was scared. Scared that her prediction would come to pass. That he'd pick up a scalpel and find the salvation he'd always found there. The concentration, the focus, the intensity.

That he'd never want to leave.

Scared that he'd say yes. To surgery. To her.

And Finn didn't like feeling scared. It reminded him too much of the perpetual fear he'd lived with during his fractured childhood—for him, for Isaac. Trying to keep him safe, to keep them together.

Fear that he'd conquered a long time ago.

And frankly it pissed him off.

'Don't think you know me,' he snarled, 'because you don't. You think because we rutted like animals...' he saw her flinch at his deliberate crudity but his adrenaline was flowing and he couldn't stop '...a few times that you know me? Read my lips.' He shoved his face close to hers and watched her hazel eyes widen. 'I don't want to be a surgeon,' he hissed. 'I don't want to work at your father's precious hospital. *I don't want to be anywhere you are.*'

Evie felt like he'd taken a bloody great sword and cleaved it right through her middle, leaving her mortally wounded. A surge of white-hot bile rose in her chest as a blinding need to strike back took hold.

'You're a liar, Finn Kennedy,' she snarled. 'And a coward to boot. And to think you once called yourself a soldier!'

Finn took a step back at the disdain and contempt in her voice. No one had ever called him a coward before. No one. And he was damned if he was going to legitimise her accusation with a response.

Evie drew in a ragged breath as Finn stormed away, her insides shaking at their exchange. At her terrible insult. At the venom in his voice. Anger she'd expected—God knew, he pretty much existed in a perpetually angry state—but vitriol? That had been cutting. A block of tangled emotions rose to mingle with the acid in her chest and her legs started to shake. The urge to crumple into a heap undulated through her muscles but she refused to succumb to it.

Not here on the veranda, at least.

On autopilot she slung her hold-all over her shoulder, found the stairs, pounded down them. Hurried down the track, his angry words chasing her, nipping at her heels. And it didn't matter that she'd given as good as she'd got, that her words had been just as harsh, it was his voice that ran through her head.

Rutted like animals.

Your father's precious hospital.

I don't want to be anywhere you're at.

It was a little early for her rendezvous with the guys—it didn't matter, she had to keep moving, do something other than think, get away from his words.

Rutted like animals.

The ocean, more rolling than pounding and surprisingly calm in some areas beneath the leaden sky, lay before her and she knew it was what she needed. To cleanse herself. Let the ocean wash the ugliness of his words away.

Rutted. Rutted. Rutted.

She took the stairs two at a time, her breath choking and catching in her throat, shaking her head to jam the audio playing on continuous loop.

Her foot hit the sand, her lungs and throat burning as breath and sob fought for the lion's share of each inhalation. She ran down to the shoreline, dropped her bag and kept

going, running into the water, not registering the cooler temperature or the depth she
quickly reached.

She just threw herself into the waves and
struck out against the ocean. Heaving in
oxygen through her nose, pulling armfuls of
water behind her as she freestyled like she
had a rocket attached to her feet.

Getting away from Finn. Away from his
words.

Away from his rejection.

She swam and swam, not looking up or
around, just hitting out at the waves as her
anger grew to match his.

Finn Kennedy was a jerk of the highest
order.

He was a misogynist. A masochist.

Bloody-minded. Arrogant. Bastard.

And she was much too good for him.

So she swam. She swam and she swam
until she couldn't swim another stroke. And
then she stopped.

She had no idea how long she'd been swimming. All she knew was her arms, legs and
lungs were screaming at her and the beach
seemed a very long way away. And the
thought of having to swim all the way back
was not a welcome one.

Damn it. Now look what he'd done.

He'd chased her right out into the middle of the bloody ocean. She sighed as she prepared to swim back.

Finn stood on the cliff top, his anxiety lessening as Evie came closer to land. Stupid fool to go out swimming by herself. The water might look calm to the untrained eye but the swell often made swimming very hard going and the tide was on the turn—always a more dangerous time to be in the water. From this vantage point he could see a rip forming close to the shore before his eyes.

And Evie was swimming right into it.

'Evie!' he called out, even though he knew it was futile all the way up here, with the wind snatching everything away.

He hit the stairs at a run, his gaze trained firmly on Evie, watching as she started to go backwards despite her forward stroke. Seeing her lift her head, her expression confused when she realised what was happening. Noting the look of panic and exhaustion as her desperate hands clawed at the water as if she was trying to gain purchase.

Thank God his raging thoughts had brought him to the cliff edge. That he'd sought the ocean to clear his head after their bitter exchange.

'Evie,' he called out again as his foot hit the sand. Still futile but coming from a place inside that kicked and burned and clawed, desperate to get the words out. 'Evie!'

It took Evie long seconds to figure out she'd been caught in a rip. And even longer seconds to stop fighting the pull at her legs and push at her body. No matter how much she kicked and bucked against the current, bands of iron seemed to pull tighter and just would not give.

Over the pounding of her heart her sluggish brain tried to remember what every Aussie kid growing up anywhere near a beach had been taught from the cradle.

Don't fight it.

Lie on your back and go with it.

Wait until it ebbs then swim parallel to the beach.

Conserve your energy.

Evie felt doomed immediately. She was already exhausted—where on earth would she find the energy to swim back again once this monstrous sucker had discharged her from its grip? She opened her eyes to glance wistfully at the rapidly receding shoreline.

And that's when she saw him.

A shirtless Finn running into the ocean,

looking right at her, his mouth open, calling to her maybe? She couldn't hear the words but just the sight of him made her heart sing. Half an hour ago she could have cheerfully murdered him but right this second he was what he'd been since that night she'd plonked herself down next to him at the gala—her everything.

She was tired and cold but suddenly she felt like everything was going to be okay and she finally relaxed and let the current sweep her along, her gaze firmly fixed on him as he threw himself into the rip and headed her way.

Her numb fingers found her bump and she whispered, 'Daddy's coming, baby.'

Finn caught up with her five minutes later as the rip swept them closer and closer to the rocky headland that divided this bay from the next.

Her lips were a pale purple and her teeth were chattering but she essentially looked in one piece and the tight fist around his heart eased a little. They weren't exactly out of the woods but she wasn't taking on water.

'You okay?' he shouted above the crash of the waves on the nearby rocks.

Evie nodded, smiling through lips that felt

frozen to her face. The man didn't even have the decency to look out of breath. 'C-cold,' she whispered.

Finn knew it would be impossible to warm her up in the water. 'I think it's weakened enough now that we can swim back. That'll get the blood flowing again.'

Evie kicked into a dog paddle and managed a feeble smile. 'Yay.'

'Are you going to be able to manage the swim?' Finn asked.

Evie looked at the distant beach and thought about her baby—their baby—depending on her to manage. 'Guess I'll have to,' she said, knowing every arm movement, every leg kick would feel like swimming through porridge.

Finn could hear her exhaustion and wondered just how far she'd make it in the swell. He scanned around. They were situated between the two bays now, with the rip spitting them out directly in front of the rocky headland—the nearest piece of terra firma.

Waves thundered where the sea met rock and Finn knew they'd be smashed mercilessly, their bones as insignificant as kindling. But the bay on the other side seemed much more sheltered and he could see a couple of areas where they might be able to gain purchase on this calmer side of the headland and pull themselves out of the water.

It would certainly be quicker and less energy-sapping than the arduous swim back to shore.

'There.' He pointed. 'We should be able to get onto those rocks. Go. I'll follow you.'

Evie felt tired just looking at the waves sloshing against the rocks. He didn't consult with her or seek agreement from her. Typical Finn—used to everyone jumping when he demanded it.

Finn frowned at her lack of activity. 'C'mon, Evie,' he said briskly. 'You're cold, you need to get out of the water.'

Evie looked back at him, his unkempt jawline and freaky blue eyes giving him a slightly crazy edge. Like he conquered rough seas and rocky headlands every day.

'Evie!' he prompted again.

Evie sighed. 'Okay, okay,' she muttered, kicking off in a pathetic type of dog paddle because anything else was beyond her.

Two slow minutes later they were almost within reach and Finn kicked ahead of her, looking for the best purchase. Finding a smooth, gently sloping rock that was almost like a ramp into the water, he reached for it. A breaker came from out of nowhere and knocked him against the surface, his ribs taking the brunt of the impact. Pain jolted him like a lightning strike and cold, salty water swept into his mouth as his breath was torn from his lungs.

Evie gasped. 'Finn!'

'I'm fine,' he grunted, gripping the surface of the rock as pain momentarily paralysed his breathing. He lay for long moments like a landed fish, gasping for air.

'Finn?'

Finn rolled on his back at an awkward angle, half on the rock, half in the water. 'I'm fine,' he said again as his lungs finally allowed the passage of a little more air. 'Here,' he said, half-sitting, the pain less now. Still, he gritted his teeth as he held out his hand. 'Grab hold, I'll pull you up.'

Evie did as she was told and in seconds she was dragged up next to him and they both half wriggled, half crawled onto flatter, water-smoothed rocks back from the edge, away from the suck and pull of the ocean.

They collapsed beside each other, dragging in air and recovering their strength. Evie shut her eyes against the feeble breaking sunlight and wished it was strong enough to warm the chill that went right down into her bones. The wind didn't help, turning the flesh on her arms and legs to goose-bumps, tightening her nipples.

Finn lay looking at the sky. His ribs hurt—for sure there was going to be a bruise there tomorrow—but now they were safe he wanted to throttle her for scaring ten years off his life. He sat up. 'Let's go.'

Evie groaned. Despite how cold she was, she just wanted to lie there and shut her eyes for a moment. 'Just a sec.'

'No,' he said standing up. 'Now. You're hypothermic. Walking will help.'

And if he stayed here with her he was going to let the adrenaline that had surged through him have free rein and it was not going to be pretty. His brain was already crowded with a hundred not-so-nice things to say to her and given that he'd already dumped on her earlier, she probably didn't need another dressing down.

He crouched beside her and grabbed her arm, pulling firmly. 'Now, Evie!'

Evie opened her eyes at the distinct crack in his tone—like a whip. She knew she should be grateful, she knew she should apologise for calling him a coward when the man had jumped into a rip to help her, but she wasn't feeling rational. She wanted a hot shower and a warm bed.

Normally she'd fantasise about snuggling into him in that bed too but he was being too crabby and today was not a normal day.

'Okay, okay,' she said, letting him drag her into a sitting position and going on autopilot as she assisted him in getting her fully upright. She leaned heavily against him as her legs almost gave out.

He cursed. 'You're freezing.'

Evie frowned at his language but nodded anyway, her teeth chattering for good measure. 'Cold,' she agreed. 'Tired.'

'Right,' he said briskly. 'Let's go. Quick march. Up and over the rocks then onto the sand then up the stairs.'

Evie groaned as her legs moved, feeling stiff and uncoordinated as if they'd had robotic implants. 'Oh, God, those bloody stairs,' she complained as Finn dragged her along.

'You'll have warmed up by then,' he said confidently.

'Oh, yes,' she mocked. 'I'll be able to sprint right up them.'

It was on the tip of Finn's tongue to snap that she'd made her own trouble but he was afraid that once he started, the fear that had gripped his gut as he'd raced down those stairs would bubble out and he'd say more stuff that he regretted, like he had earlier today.

So he didn't say anything, just coaxed, bullied and cajoled her every step over the headland, gratified to see her become more co-ordinated and less irrational as her body warmed up. When they reached sand he jogged ahead of her to where her bag had been discarded on the beach, took out her fluffy dry towel and jogged back to her, wrapping her in it.

'You must be cold too,' Evie protested as she sank into its warm folds.

'I'm fine,' he dismissed.

Somehow they made it to the top of the stairs and into the homestead and Finn was pushing Evie into the bathroom and turning the hot shower on and ordering her in. She'd never been more grateful for Finn being his bossy, crabby self.

Thirty minutes later Evie was tucked up in her bed and drifting off to sleep on a blissfully warm cloud when Finn barged in, carrying a tray.

'Drink this,' he ordered plonking a steaming mug of something on her bedside table along with a huge slab of chocolate cake on a delicate plate with a floral border. 'Reginald insists,' he said.

Evie struggled to sit up, every muscle in

her body protesting the movement. 'Well, if Reginald insists…'

She propped herself against the headrest, drawing her knees up as she reached for the mug. The aroma of chocolate seduced her, making her stomach growl and her mouth fill with saliva, and she was suddenly ravenous.

She sighed as her first sip of the hot sweet milk coated the inside of her mouth and sent her taste buds into rapture. Finn, dressed in a T-shirt and jeans, prowled around the end of her bed, slapping the tray against his legs, and she tried her best to ignore him as she reached for the cake.

Finn paced as Evie ate, reliving their moments in the ocean, still feeling edgy from the hit of adrenaline. He'd tried not to think of the hundred things that could have gone wrong when he'd been in the water and trying to get her back to the house, but the minute the bathroom door had shut and he'd known she was truly safe, reaction had well and truly set in.

They'd been lucky. *She'd* been lucky. He wondered if she had a clue how close she'd come to being a drowning statistic. The thought sent a chill up his spine.

As much as she was a pain in his butt,

the thought of her not being around was unthinkable.

Did she not realise how precious life was?

Had growing up with that damn silver spoon in her mouth blinded her to the perils mere mortals faced every day?

Bloody little princess!

His ribs grabbed and moaned at him with every footfall, stoking his anger at her stupidity higher and higher.

Evie had eaten half of the cake before his silent skulking finally got on her last nerve. 'Why don't you just say it, Finn?'

Finn stopped mid-pace and looked at her. Her hair was still damp from her near-death experience in an unfriendly ocean and despite her obvious exhaustion she looked so damned imperious and defiant he wanted to put her over his knee and spank her. He threw the tray on the bed.

'What the devil were you doing, swimming by yourself? You could have been swept out to sea, dashed on the rocks, drowned from exhaustion, frozen to death or been eaten by a bloody shark!'

Evie blinked at the litany of things that could have befallen her. They'd lurked in her mind as the current had dragged her further and further away from the shore but she'd tried not to give them any power. Trust Finn to shove them in her face.

Did he really think she needed them spelled out?

Did he think she hadn't collapsed on her butt in the shower, shaking from head to toe at the what-ifs? That she hadn't thought about how she'd not only put her life at risk but the life of their unborn child? She'd never been more grateful to feel the energetic movements of her baby as she'd stripped off her clothes in the shower.

'I know,' she said quietly

But Finn had started pacing again and was, apparently, on a roll. 'And none of us would have known. You'd just suddenly be missing, just…gone.' He clicked his fingers in the air. 'And there'd be hundreds of people everywhere out there, looking for you. Combing the bush and the ocean, and your sisters would be frantic and your father would want to shut this place down and wouldn't rest until Ethan—' He stopped and glared at her. '*A good man doing good things* was nailed to a wall but what would you care? You'd be dead.'

Evie dragged in a rough breath at the passion of his mesmerising speech and his heated gaze that swept over her as if he could see down to her bones.

And what about you, Finn? How would it make you feel?

It hadn't been her goal to scare an admission out of him but his tirade gave her a little hope. Would he be this het up about someone he didn't have feelings for?

'I'm sorry,' she apologised.

'Well, that's not enough!' He twisted to resume his pacing but the abrupt movement jarred through his injury and he cursed under his breath, movement impossible as he grabbed automatically at his ribs with one hand and the wooden framework at the foot of the bed with the other.

Evie sat forward. 'Finn?' He didn't answer, just stood sucking in air, his eyes squeezed shut, his hand splinting his chest. 'Finn!'

'I'm fine,' he snapped.

Evie peeled back the cover and crawled to the end of the bed on her hands and knees. 'You are not,' she said as she drew level with him. 'Let me look,' she said, reaching for his shirt.

Finn stood upright, batting her hand away. 'I said I'm fine, damn it!'

She was wearing a baggy T-shirt and loose cotton shorts that came to just above her knee and she smelled fresh and soapy from the shower and she was so close he wanted to drag her into his arms and assure himself that she really was okay.

But he also wanted to kiss her hard and lose himself in her for a while, and he was more than pleased there was a wooden bed end as a barrier between them.

'Finn, I'm a doctor, remember?'

'So am I.'

She nodded. 'Which is exactly why you shouldn't be diagnosing yourself.'

'It's just a bruise,' he dismissed.

She reached for his shirt, laying her hand against his chest. 'Why don't you let me be the judge of that?' she murmured.

Her palm print seared into his chest and shot his resolve down in flames. He knew he should step back, walk away, but she was lifting his shirt and she was safe and well and so very close, looking like Evie and smelling like her and reminding him of all the times he'd seen her in the hallways at the Harbour looking at him with that aloofness that didn't fool him and making him want her even more and he couldn't make himself resist her.

Not after today.

Evie gasped at the ugly blue black bruise on his side, her fingers automatically tracing its ugly outline. 'Bloody hell, Finn,' she murmured.

But already her fingers were becoming methodical, prodding, shutting her eyes as she fell into a familiar routine. She pushed gently all around the injured area, feeling Finn's abdominal muscles tense, hearing the harsh suck of his breath.

'Sorry,' she murmured, opening her eyes, her own breath catching at their proximity, at the intensity in his gaze. 'Can't feel or hear any crepitus,' she said, her voice unsteady.

'That's because they're not broken,' he said.

Evie nodded, her breath thick in her throat as her fingers lightly stroked the bruised tissue, exploring the dips of his ribs. 'You should get an X-ray tomorrow when we get back to the Harbour.'

Finn nodded as the light caress of her cool fingers soothed and inflamed all at once. 'Maybe.'

Evie smiled. She guessed his ribs *must* be bad for him to sort of comply so easily. She dropped her hand but he didn't move away and she didn't want him to. They were close enough for her to lay her head on his chest, have him put his arms around her.

Close enough to tell him about the baby.

The silence stretched but she just couldn't get the words out. And she needed him to come back to Sydney. Not disappear.

But she had to say something. Because if she didn't she was going to kiss him and then they'd be on the bed because a kiss was never enough with Finn and he'd find out then for sure.

'Sorry for calling you a coward,' she murmured. 'You're not. Not in the physical sense, anyway. You certainly proved that today.'

Finn grunted. Only Evie could call him an emotional coward and couch it as a compliment. 'I'm sorry for what I said too. I…'

He broke off. He what? He did want to be a surgeon? He did want to be near her? The truth was he'd spoken his mind. But he'd never wanted to hurt her with it. To throw his words at her like they were poisonous darts.

'You what?' she prompted as his unfinished sentence hung in the air.

Finn shook his head, his gaze dropping to Evie's mouth. 'You drive me crazy.'

Evie pulled her bottom lip between her teeth. 'I know.'

Finn felt the movement jolt all the way down to his groin. 'Damn it,' he muttered, reaching for her, sliding his hand under her damp hair at the back of her neck, pulling her head closer as he closed the gap from his side, claiming her mouth on a tortured groan.

'Damn it, damn it, damn it,' he muttered against her lips, as she whimpered and the urge to hurdle the barrier between them took hold and he pushed his other hand into her hair and her mouth opened as his moved against hers and he kissed her hard and deep and hungry, every ragged breath tearing through his ribcage.

A loud knock thundered against her door and he pulled away, gasping. They both were.

'Evie? Evie? Are you okay?'

Finn clutched his chest again as he took a step back, every nerve ending on fire, every cell begging him to get closer, to get looser, to get naked.

His gaze never left her face as he slowly backed even further away, her moist mouth and glazed expression slugging him straight in the groin, begging him to come nearer.

His back bumped gently against the door. 'She's fine, Ethan,' he called.

Then he turned the doorhandle and admitted his friend. And a massive slice of sanity.

CHAPTER FOUR

ON MONDAY MORNING at eight-ten precisely Finn picked up the scalpel and knew Evie was right.

He couldn't not be a surgeon.

He'd been wasting his time, his talent, his future at *Beach Haven* when his true calling was right here—surgery.

Damn it!

As he worked methodically through the steps of the quadruple bypass, as familiar to him as his own breath, the fact that the man on the table was one of the world's richest men faded to black.

Everything faded to black.

It was just him, an open chest and a beating heart. Cutting into the pericardium, harvesting the veins, putting the patient on bypass, clamping the aorta, starting the clock, stopping the heart, grafting the veins beyond the coronary artery blockages, restarting the heart, closing up.

One hundred per cent focused. One hundred per cent absorbed.

Coming out of the zone as he stood back and peeled his gloves off, a little dazed still, as if he'd been in a trance. Registering again the smell of the mask in his nose, the trill and ping of machinery, the strains of Mozart which had been Prince Khalid's music of choice. The murmur of voices around him as they prepared to transfer the patient to ICU.

'Thanks, everyone,' he acknowledged, surprised momentarily that he hadn't been alone.

Nothing had touched him as his fingers and brain had worked in tandem. Evie had been forgotten Isaac had been forgotten. The gnawing hunger of a crappy childhood forgotten.

Just him and the knife.

Taking it all away. Centring him.

And as the outside world started to percolate in through his conscious state, he knew he needed it again.

Damn it!

Finn was surprised to see Evie at the canteen half an hour later when he dropped by to get something to eat on his way to check on Khalid in ICU. Surprised who she was with, anyway. She was sitting with Marco D'Avello and they looked deep in conversation. Marco reached out and touched her hand and Finn was annoyed at the quick burn of acid in his chest. Marco was married—happily married—to Emily and they'd not long had their first child.

What the hell was he doing, touching Evie in the middle of the canteen where everyone could see them?

He hadn't pegged Marco as the straying kind.

Or Evie as a home-wrecker, for that matter.

And even though he knew that wasn't what was going on because he *knew* Evie, it irritated him nonetheless. And not everyone sitting in the canteen would be so forgiving.

He turned away as he placed his order but a sudden short burst of laughter from Evie had him looking back, and suddenly she was looking up and in his direction and her smile died, and for a moment they both just looked at each other before Evie stood up and headed his way.

The woman behind the counter handed Finn his sandwich and drink and he headed for the door.

He didn't want or need any Evie Lockheart chit-chat.

'Finn,' Evie called as he walked out the door, her legs hurrying to catch up. Drat the man—she just wanted to ask him about the surgery. 'Finn. Wait!' she called again as she stepped outside. She watched as he faltered and his shoulders seemed to fall before he slowly turned to face her.

She was in baggy work scrubs—her long, lean legs outlined with each step towards him, and he averted his eyes as he waited for her to catch him up before he resumed his trajectory.

'How'd it go?' Evie asked as she fell into step beside him.

'Fine.'

Evie waited for him to elaborate. He didn't. 'Prince Khalid came through it okay?'

He nodded. 'I'm just going to check on him now.'

They walked some more in silence and Evie could have gleefully strangled him. 'Well?' she demanded when she couldn't wait for him to be forthcoming any longer. 'How'd it feel?' she asked. 'Was it good to be back?'

Finn stopped and shoved his hands on his hips. 'Yes. Was that what you wanted to hear? That you were right? That it felt like

I was coming home? Well, it did. And after I've been to the ICU I'm heading up to Eric Frobisher's office to get myself back on the OR schedule. Eric, who is an arse and will make a huge song and dance over the *inconvenience* of it all, even though he knows I'm the best damn cardiothoracic surgeon in the country, just because he can. Are you satisfied?'

Evie wanted to be satisfied. Her heart was tapping out a jig and emotion, light and airy, bloomed in her chest. If he was here then maybe there was a chance for them. Maybe with the baby in the mix, Finn would eventually admit what she knew was in his heart.

But she didn't want him to feel trapped.

'I'm glad that you're staying. But I don't want you to be miserable.'

'Well, you can't have it both ways, Princess Evie. You can have me here doing what I do best, what I need to do, but if you want me to be whistling in the corridors and singing to bluebirds as they land on my shoulder, that isn't going to happen.'

He dropped his hands and started walking again towards the lifts.

'You don't have to work here,' she called after his back. What was the point if he just came to resent her more? 'You could do this anywhere. You could walk into any hospital in this country and name your price.'

It was a startling reality for her but Evie knew that a man like Finn had to operate. Even if it meant doing it somewhere else. Didn't they say if you loved someone you had to set them free?

Finn turned again. He knew that. He'd done nothing but turn the conundrum over and over in his brain for the last half an hour. He'd trawled through his many options but had discarded each one. Partly because Sydney Harbour Hospital had the best cardiothoracic department in the country, partly because Evie was here and he just didn't seem to be able to stay away, but mostly because it felt like home. It was the longest he'd ever stayed anywhere and deep down Finn was still an eight-year-old boy desperate for the stability of the familiar.

'I only work at the best,' he said impatiently, knowing it was only a half-truth and feeling like a coward as she looked at him with her clear hazel gaze. 'Sydney Harbour Hospital is the best.'

He marched to the lift and pushed the button. She followed. The empty lift arrived promptly. He got on.

She followed.

And because he was angry that she was still right beside him and that she was always going to be around as long as he was here, smoothing away at his edges and his resistance like bloody Chinese water torture, he lashed out at the first thing that entered his head.

'I didn't realise you and Marco D'Avello were such pals.'

Evie frowned at the slight accusation in his voice, nervous that he might connect the dots. 'I'm sorry?'

'You need to be careful. You know how easily gossip starts in a place like this.'

Evie blinked as his implication became clear. Clearly no dots to worry about! 'Don't be ridiculous,' she spluttered.

Finn held up a hand in surrender. 'I really don't care what you do, Evie, or who you do it with,' he lied, 'but maybe you might like to consider his wife and their newborn baby and how gossip might affect them.'

Evie was momentarily speechless. Which turned to outrage pretty quickly. She wasn't sure if it was because of what he was suggesting or the fact that he really didn't seem to give a fig if it was the truth or not.

That she might actually be sleeping with Marco D'Avello.

Who was married!

The lift pinged as they arrived on the third floor and the doors opened. 'Is that what you think?' she asked as he walked out. She stepped out too just as two nurses appeared, grabbing the lift as the doors started to shut. 'That Marco and I are…having some kind of affair?' she hissed as the doors shut behind them.

Finn sighed at the injury in her voice and quashed the little niggle of irritation that had pecked at his brain since he'd witnessed the canteen hand squeeze. 'Of course not, Evie. But in this place, where gossip is a second language, you can bet that others will…that's all I'm saying.'

Evie glared at him. Wanted to tell him he was being preposterous but she knew it to be true. How much gossip had she heard about herself over the years? In her first year it had been about what a stuck-up cow she was, breaking poor Stuart's heart, thinking she was too good for him even though he'd broken her heart when she'd discovered he only wanted her for her family name and connections.

And in this last year or so endless reams of gossip about her and Finn.

Evie felt herself deflate like a balloon as

all the fight oozed out of her. 'Yes. People do like to talk, don't they?'

Finn shrugged. 'Well, they're going to talk anyway. Best not to feed them too much ammunition—that's my philosophy.'

Evie blinked. 'You've done nothing but feed them ammunition the entire time you've been here. Sleeping with any pretty young thing that batted her eyelashes at you.'

Even her. Not that she'd ever batted her eyelashes.

He grinned. 'It stopped them talking about my injury, though, didn't it?'

Evie grinned back at his unashamed admission—she couldn't help herself. He suddenly seemed years younger than his trademark stubbly jawline portrayed and it was rare to share such a moment with him. He was always so intense—to see him amused was breathtaking.

Suddenly Evie felt back on an even keel. Enough to begin a dialogue about the subject she'd been avoiding. 'Do you think we can find some time this week to talk?' she asked tentatively.

Finn felt the bubble of happiness that had percolated from nowhere burst with a resounding pop. *A talk* sounded as inviting as root-canal treatment.

He eyed her warily. 'I don't like to talk.'

Evie nodded. 'I've noticed.'

'Nothing's changed just because I'm back, Evie.'

She steeled herself against the ominous warning. It would do her well to take heed.

Finn Kennedy was one hard nut to crack.

'I know,' she rushed to assure him. 'It's not about that. About us.'

Not strictly speaking anyway.

She crossed her fingers behind her back. 'It's…something else.' She stopped and wondered if it sounded like the complete hash it was. 'It's to do with work…'

It was. *Sort of.* Her career was going to have to take a back seat for a while. His would be affected too if he wanted to be involved with the baby.

She watched his frown deepen. Why did she have to fall for a man who was always so suspicious? 'Look, it's complicated, okay? Can you just say yes? Then I'll promise not to bother you again.'

Finn wasn't keen on *a talk*. In his experience women's talks involved rings and dresses and happily ever afters. But it was work related… and the payoff sounded pretty damn good to him.

Never being bothered by her again was an opportunity he couldn't pass up.

It was a futile hope, of course, because he dreamed about her too bloody much to ever fully realise that blissful state of Evie-lessness and every time he saw her a very distinct, very unevolved, caveman urge seemed to overcome him.

But if she could do her bit then he could master the rest. He was used to it.

'After Khalid's discharge?' he suggested. 'A few days? At Pete's?'

Evie slowly exhaled her pent-up breath. 'Thank you.'

Finn nodded. 'I'll let you know.'

He didn't wait for her to answer. Just turned away, his mind already shifting gears.

After some rhythm complications, it was Friday afternoon before Khalid was discharged to a penthouse suite at one of the city's most luxurious hotels. It was top secret but Finn knew and Khalid had his number. Along with round-the-clock private nurses, Finn was confident the prince would have a very nice convalescence with a world-class view.

He'd seen Evie around over the intervening days—with just one VIP patient on his books, he wasn't exactly flush with things to do. In fact, glimpses of her here, there and everywhere were driving him more than a little nutty. And always, it seemed, she was deep in conversation with Marco. By the end of the week he was starting to wonder if perhaps there *was* something going on with them after all.

His idleness was driving him spare—giving him too much time to think. At *Beach Haven* it had been what he'd needed—but back in amongst the rush and hurry of *the Harbour* he needed to be busy. Eric, the CEO, had been the superior jerk he'd predicted and had refused to put Finn back on the surgical roster until after their VIP had been discharged.

But, as of Monday, he was back. Which would give him a lot less time to wonder about what Evie and Marco were up to.

To wonder about Evie full stop.

The prospect of *the talk* had kept her front and centre all week—with no surgery to do and just Khalid to see, there'd been nothing else to occupy his brain. He pulled his mobile phone out of his pocket as he made his way to his outpatient rooms. It was time to get it out of the way.

Check it off his list.

Start the new week with a clean slate.

And it was an opportunity to lay down some ground rules with Evie. They couldn't go on the way they had been prior to him leaving. He was different now—his injury was healed. He didn't need anyone's sympathy or pity or to cover for his lapses.

If they were going to co-exist peacefully in this hospital he had to start as he meant to go on.

Without Evie.

Evie breathed a sigh of relief as the electronic noise of the monitor grew fainter as the last patient from the pile-up on the motorway was whisked off to Theatre. They'd been frantic for hours and between the adrenaline buzz, the noise pollution and the baby dancing the rumba inside her she had a massive headache.

She could hear the soft plaintive beep of another alarm in the empty cubicle and it nibbled at her subconscious like fingernails down a chalk board. 'Where the hell is that coming from?' she asked irritably as her stomach growled and the baby kicked.

She looked around at the electronic gadgetry vital in a modern emergency department. The alarm wasn't one she was familiar with as she approached the bank of monitors and pumps.

'It's the new CO2 monitor,' Mia di Angelo, her ex-flatmate and fellow emergency physician, said. 'It can't be on charge.'

Evie scanned the machines for an unfamiliar one. She hated it when they got new equipment. It was great to keep their department up to date and stocked with the latest and greatest but it was hell assimilating all the new alarms and buttons.

When she located the unfamiliar piece of equipment with its little yellow flashing light she followed the cord at the back and noticed it trailing on the floor instead of being plugged into the power supply at the back of the cubicle. She squeezed in behind, not such an easy job any more, and the baby let her know it did not like being constricted by a swift one-two jab.

She sucked in a breath, her hand automatically going to her belly in a soothing motion as she bent over, picked up the plug from the floor and pushed it into the socket.

Instead of the instant peace she was hoping for, a loud sizzle followed by some sparks and the pungent smell of burnt electrical wiring rent the air. The point where her fingers touched the plug tingled then burned, a painful jolt cramped up her arm and knocked her backwards onto her butt.

'Evie!' Mia gasped rushing to her friend's side. 'Are you okay?'

Evie blinked, too dazed for a moment to fully understand what had happened. All she was aware of was a pain in her finger and the sudden stillness of the baby.

'What's wrong?' Evie heard Luca's voice. He was Mia's husband and head of the department.

'Help me get her up,' Mia said. 'She got an electric shock from the pump.'

Evie felt arms half pulling, half guiding her into a standing position. 'Evie, talk to me. Are you okay?' Mia was saying, inspecting the tiny white mark on Evie's index finger.

'Let's get her on a monitor,' Luca was saying as his fingers palpated the pulse at her wrist.

Suddenly she broke out of her daze. 'No.'

She shook her head. The baby. It was so, so still. She needed to see Marco. She had to know if the shock had affected the baby.

She had to know now.

'I'm fine,' she assured them, breaking out of their hold. 'Really I am.'

Mia frowned and folded her arms. 'You just got a zap that knocked you on your butt. You should be monitored for a while.'

Evie shook her head again and forced a

smile onto her face even though it felt like it was going to crack into a thousand pieces as concern for the baby sky-rocketed with every single stationary second. 'I'm fine. I'm in the middle of a hospital. If I start to feel unwell, I'll let you know.'

Luca nodded. 'Her pulse is steady.'

Mia grabbed Evie's hand. 'This could do with a burns consult in case it's worse than it looks. It'll definitely need dressing.'

Evie thought quickly. 'Yes. Good idea. It's burns clinic today, right? I'll pop in and see if they can squeeze me in.'

'I'll come with you,' Mia said.

'Status epilepticus two minutes out,' a nurse said to them as she dashed past.

And then the distant strains of a siren, a beautiful, beautiful siren, made itself known, and Evie had never been more grateful to hear the wretched noise.

'You can't,' Evie said. 'You're needed here. You both are. I'll be fine,' she assured them again, a surge of desperation to get away, to get to Marco, making her feel impotent.

'Okay,' Mia acquiesced. 'But I want to see you after you get back.'

Evie nodded. 'Absolutely.'

By the time she scurried up to the outpatient department ten minutes later Evie was frantic. The baby hadn't moved and an ominous black cloud hovered over her head. When she'd been hypothermic in the middle of the ocean her brain had been too sluggish to think of the implications for the baby. But today all her mental faculties were intact and totally freaking her out as all the horrible possibilities marched one by one through her mind.

She was on the verge of tears when she finally located Marco, who wasn't in his rooms but was chatting to a midwife in the long corridor that ran behind the outpatients department.

'Marco,' she called.

He looked up and smiled at her, his joy quickly dying as he saw the distress on her face. He strode over to her.

'Evie,' he said with that lovely lilt of his, his hands grasping her upper arms, a frown marring his classically handsome face. He could see she was about to crumple and led her away from the busy thoroughfare into the nearby cleaning closet. It wasn't very roomy and the door was chocked open but it was more private than outside. 'What is wrong?'

'I think the baby might be dead,' she whispered, choking on a sob as she buried her face in his chest.

* * *

Finn scrolled through his contacts on his phone as he stepped out of the lift and headed for the outpatients department. He wanted to spend some time looking at the case notes for his theatre list on Monday. He found Evie's number and hit the button as he entered the department.

His gaze wandered across to the corridor on the far side as he waited for her to pick up and that's when he spotted them. Evie and Marco alone in some kind of supply cupboard—embracing. He fell back a little, shocked by the image, watching them from just outside the department as they pulled apart slightly and Evie fumbled in her scrubs pocket and pulled out her phone.

'Hello?'

Finn didn't say anything for a moment, trying to decide how he should play it. 'It's me,' he said, watching her as she stayed in the shelter of Marco's body, his arm around her shoulder. 'I'm free for that talk now.'

Evie looked up at Marco as she grappled with a vortex of emotions

Now? He wanted to talk now?

'Er…I can't right now… I'm busy.'

Finn raised an eyebrow. Icy fingers crept around his heart and he leant against the nearby wall. 'Emergency a little crazy at the moment?'

Evie nodded, grabbing the excuse he had thrown her with glee. 'Certifiable.'

The fingers squeezed down hard. 'I could come down there and wait for you,' he suggested.

Alarm raced along Evie's nerve endings. 'No, no,' she said. 'I'll give you a ring when it settles and I can meet you across at Pete's.'

'Okay,' he murmured.

'Bye.'

Finn blinked at her hasty hang-up and to torture himself a little further he watched as Marco drew her against his chest and hugged her again before walking her to his rooms, his arm firmly around her waist.

He had absolutely no idea what the hell was going on with those two but he had every intention of finding out! She'd been pretty convincing in her mortification at his inference that she and Marco were *sleeping together* a few days ago but maybe she was protesting too much? Maybe there was more to Marco and Evie than she was letting on?

His heart pounded as bile burned in his chest and acid flowed through his veins. He pushed off the wall and headed in their direction.

'Finn Kennedy, well, I'll be. I heard you were back.'

Finn stopped in mid-stride to greet Sister Enid Kenny, nurse in charge of Outpatients for about a hundred years and a true Sydney Harbour Hospital icon. She was large and matronly and no one, not even the great Finn Kennedy, messed with Enid Kenny.

If she wanted to chat, you stopped and chatted.

Unfortunately for him, as he looked over her shoulder at the closed door of Marco's office, she was in a very chatty mood.

Evie was so relived she'd agreed to the ultrasound as she watched her baby—her baby boy—move around on the screen. Marco had been trying to convince her to have one all week but part of her had wanted to break the news to Finn before having an ultrasound, which she'd been hoping he would want to attend.

But after her scare just listening to the heartbeat wasn't going to cut it. She needed to see him. To watch him move. To reassure herself fully. To count his fingers and toes, to see the chambers of his heart, the hemispheres of his brain.

To know everything was perfect.

Marco was very thorough doing measurements and pointing out all the things any radiographer would have and Evie felt the gut wrenching worry and the threatening hysteria ease as her little boy did indeed seem perfect.

'Can I hear the heartbeat one more time?' Evie asked.

Marco chuckled. 'But of course.'

He flicked a switch on the ultrasound machine and the room filled with the steady *whop, whop, whop* of a robust heartbeat.

Neither of them expected the door to suddenly crash open or for Finn to be standing there, glowering at them and demanding to know what the devil was going on.

Evie was startled at the loud intrusion. 'Finn,' she whispered.

Marco turned calmly in his chair. 'Welcome, Dr Kennedy. You're just in time to meet your son,' he said.

It took Finn a moment or two to compute the scene before his eyes. The lights down low. Evie lying on the examination bed, her scrub top pulled up, a very distinctive bump protruding and covered in goo. Marco's hand holding an ultrasound probe low down on Evie's belly. A grainy image of a foetus turning somersaults on the screen.

And the steady thump of a strong heartbeat.

Finn looked at Evie and shoved his hands on his hips. 'What the hell…?' he demanded.

Marco looked at Evie as he removed the probe and reached for some wipes. 'I think I should leave you and Finn to talk, yes?' he murmured as he methodically removed every trace of the conduction gel.

Evie sat up, dragging her top down as she did so. Finn stood aside as Marco passed him, flipping on the light as he went and shutting the door after him.

'You're pregnant?' he demanded, his own heartbeat roaring through his ears at the stunning turn of events. He'd half expected to barge in and find she and Marco doing the wild thing on the desk. He'd never expected this.

Evie nodded. 'Yes.'

Her quiet affirmative packed all the power of a sucker punch to his solar plexus. 'This is what you wanted to talk about?'

'Yes.'

He shook his head as all the control he'd fought for over the years started to disintegrate before him, unravelling like a spool of cotton.

His breath felt tight. His jaw clenched. His pulse throbbed through his veins, tapping out *no, no, no* against his temple.

'No.'

He couldn't be a father. He just couldn't. He was selfish and arrogant and egotistical. He was busy. He was dedicated to his job. He hadn't grown up in any home worth a damn and the one person who'd been entrusted to his care had died in his arms.

He was damaged goods. Seen too much that had hardened him. Made him cynical. Jaded.

Not father material.

Most days he didn't even know how to be a normal, functioning human being—he was just going through the motions.

How on earth could he be a decent father?

He looked at her watching him, wariness in her hazel eyes. But hope as well. And something else. The same thing he always saw there when she looked at him—belief.

She had no idea who he really was.

He steeled his heart against the image that seemed to be ingrained on his retinas—his baby on an ultrasound screen.

'You have to get an abortion.'

Evie flinched at the ice in his tone. It wasn't anything she hadn't thought about herself in those days when she'd lived in a space where denying the baby even existed had been preferable to facing the truth. But she'd felt him move now, seen him sucking his thumb on the screen just a few minutes ago, and even if she hadn't already decided against it and it had been possible at this advanced stage in her pregnancy, she knew she could never do what Finn was asking.

'I'm twenty-one weeks.'

Finn opened his mouth to dispute it but the evidence of his own eyes started to filter in. The size of her belly and the size of the baby on the screen and then some quick maths in his head all confirmed her gestation.

He groped for Marco's desk as the import of her words hit home.

There could be no abortion.

There would be a baby.

He was going to be a father.

'Why didn't you tell me?'

Evie swung her legs over the edge of the couch. 'Because you went away and I spent a long, *long* time in denial. And, honestly, I think because part of me knew you'd demand what you just demanded and even though I'd thought about it myself, a part of me wanted to put it beyond reach. For both of us. And then the longer you go...' she shrugged. '...the harder it gets.'

'You've just spent two weeks with me at *Beach Haven*. You could have told me then.'

'I almost did but...' She looked at him staring at her like she'd just been caught with state secrets instead of a bun in the oven. 'You're not very approachable, Finn.'

He looked at her for a long moment. 'I don't know how to be a father.'

Evie sucked in a breath at the bleakness in his blue eyes. He suddenly looked middle-aged. 'You think I know how to be a mother?' she asked. 'My mother was an absent alcoholic. Not exactly a stellar role model.'

Finn snorted. She had no idea. Her poor-little-rich-girl upbringing had been a walk in the park compared to his. 'I think you'll figure it out.'

'I think you will, too,' she said, feeling suddenly desperate to connect with him. To make him understand that she knew it was daunting. But they could do it.

Finn's pager beeped and he was grateful for the distraction as he absently reached for it and checked the message on the screen. It was Khalid.

'I have to go,' he said.

He needed to think. To get away. Life events had robbed him of a lot of choices and now even the choice not to burden some poor child with his emotionally barren existence had been snatched away.

'Okay.' She nodded, pushing down the well of emotion that was threatening as she watched him turn away from her.

He needed time and she had to give him that. It had taken *her* months to adjust and accept and she wasn't Finn. A man who didn't express emotion well and never let anyone close.

She had to give him space to come to terms with it.

So she sat there like a dummy as he walked out the door, despite how very, very much she wanted to call him back.

CHAPTER FIVE

FINN WOKE UP at nine on Saturday morning, his head throbbing from one too many hits of his very expensive malt whisky the previous night.

It had been a good while since he'd overdone the top-shelf stuff. For years he'd used it to dull the physical pain from his injuries but since his recovery and his move to *Beach Haven* he'd only ever indulged in the odd beer or two.

He'd forgotten how it could feel like a mule had kicked you in the head the next day. Which might actually be worth it if it had come with some sort of clarity.

It hadn't.

Just a thumping headache and the very real feeling that he'd woken up in hell.

He stared at the ceiling as the same three words from last night repeated in his head— *Evie is pregnant.* Each word pounded like a battering ram against the fortified shell surrounding his heart with a resounding boom.

Evie. *Boom!* Is. *Boom!* Pregnant. *Boom!*

He was going to be a father. Some tiny little defenceless human being with his DNA was going to make its arrival in four short months. He was going to be *Daddy*.

Whether he liked it or not.

And it scared the hell out of him. Being a parent—*a good parent*—required things life just hadn't equipped him with. Like compassion, empathy, love.

There'd been so little love in his life. From the moment his mother had abandoned him and Isaac to a childhood in institutions to his regimented life in the army, ruled by discipline and authority, love had been non-existent. Sure, he'd loved and protected Isaac and Isaac had loved him, but it had been a very lonely island in a vast sea of indifference.

Add to that the slow fossilising of his emotions to deal with the horror and injuries witnessed in far-flung battlefields and the death knell to any errant tendrils of love and tenderness that might still have existed when Isaac had died in his arms and the product was the man he was today.

Ten years since that horrifying day and still he felt numb. Blank. Barren.

Emotionally void.

He hadn't loved Lydia, his brother's widow, with whom he'd had a totally messed up affair and who had needed him to love her no matter how screwed up it had been at the time.

He operated with the cold, clinical precision of a robot. Always seeing the part, never seeing the whole. Totally focussed. Never allowing himself to think about the person whose heart he held in his hands or the love that heart was capable of. Just doing the job. And doing it damn well.

He hadn't felt anything for any of the women he'd slept with. They had just been pleasant distractions. Something different to take to bed instead of a bottle of Scotch. A momentary diversion.

Apart from Evie. Whom he'd pushed and pushed and pushed away and who knew what he was like but refused to give up anyway. Who could look right past his rubbish and see deep inside to the things he kept hidden.

Evie, who was having his baby.

A baby he didn't know how to love.

A sudden knock at his door stomped through his head like a herd of stampeding elephants and he groaned out loud. He wanted to yell to whoever it was to go away but was afraid he might have a stroke if he did. If he just lay here, maybe Evie would think he'd already gone out.

Because that knock had the exact cadence of a pissed-off woman.

It came again followed by, 'Finn? Finn!'

Lydia? Wrong pissed-off woman.

'Finn Kennedy, open this bloody door now. Don't make me get my key out!'

Finn rolled out of bed. It wasn't the smoothest exit from his bed he'd ever executed but considering he felt like he was about to die, the fact he could walk at all was a miracle.

'Coming,' he called as the knock came again, wincing as it drove nails into his brain.

He wrenched open the door just as he heard a metallic scratching from the other side. His brother's widow, a petite redhead, stood on the doorstep glowering at him, hands on hips.

'You look like hell,' she said.

He grunted. 'I feel like hell.'

'Right,' she said, striding past him into his apartment. 'Coffee first, I think. Then you can tell me what happened to get you into this state.'

Finn was tempted to throw her out. But he really, really needed coffee.

Fifteen minutes later he was inhaling the aroma of the same Peruvian Arabica beans

Lydia had brought him the last time she'd come for a flying visit and he hadn't touched since. Grinding beans was way too much trouble, no matter how good they were. He took a sip of coffee and shut his eyes as his pulse gave a little kick.

His home phone rang from the direction of his bedroom and he ignored it as he felt the coffee slowly reviving him. Khalid only had his mobile number and everything else could just wait.

Lydia waited until he'd taken a few more sips before pinning him with that direct look of hers. She'd come a long way since the broken woman he'd comforted a decade ago. In his own grief and in the midst of their screwy relationship he had judged her harshly for that, for what he'd perceived as weakness, but she had come out the other side a much stronger person.

'Spill,' she said.

Finn thought about playing dumb but the truth was that Lydia was one of the few people who really understood how he ticked. She'd been the one who'd moved on from their half-hearted affair when she'd seen it had been perpetuating an unhealthy co-dependence. The strange mix of relief and regret at its ending had confused him but she'd never left him completely and as his one tangible link to Isaac he'd been grateful for her watchful eye and bossy persona.

'Evie's pregnant.'

Lydia blinked. 'Oh.'

Finn took another sip of his coffee. 'Indeed.'

'It's yours?'

Finn nodded. It wasn't something he'd questioned for a moment. 'A little boy.'

'Oh,' Lydia said again, hiding a smile as she sipped at her coffee.

Finn frowned. 'Are you smiling?'

Lydia shook her head, feigning a serious expression. 'Absolutely not.'

'This is not funny.'

Her shaking became more vigorous. 'Not funny at all.'

Finn plonked his mug on the coffee table and raked his hands through his hair; his chest felt tight and his heart raced. He blamed the coffee rather than what he suspected it actually was—sheer panic.

Lydia didn't understand.

Except she did.

His hands trembled as he looked at her with bleak eyes that had seen too much hate. 'I'm too damaged for a baby, Lyd.'

Lydia's smile disappeared in an instant and

she reached out her hand to cover his. 'Maybe this is just what you need to help you heal?' she murmured.

He shook her hand away—how could he gamble that on the life of an innocent child? 'I never wanted a baby. This wasn't my choice.'

'Well, we don't always get what we want in life, do we, Finn? You know that better than anyone. So you didn't get a say? Too bad—it's here, it's happening. And guess what, you do get a choice about what you do now.'

Finn stared at her incredulously. 'What? *Be a father*?'

'Yes,' she nodded. 'Be a father.'

Finn shook his head as his chest grew tighter, practically constricting his chest. 'No.'

'Be the father you always wanted.'

Finn shook his head. 'I never wanted a father.'

Lydia gave him a stern look. 'Isaac told me, Finn. He told me how you wished every night for a father to come and take you both away from it all. That you'd tell him stories about him picking you up and taking you to Luna Park for the day and a ferry on the harbour and then back to his house by the sea. You can't go back and fix that, but you do get a chance to start over.'

Lydia stood, swooping his empty mug off the table. 'You want your son to not have a father either? To miss out on such a vital ingredient in his childhood? To dream every night of you coming and taking him out to Luna Park and for a ride on the ferry and to live by the sea? A boy needs a father, Finn.'

'He needs a mother more.'

She shook her head. 'No, he needs a mother *as well*.'

Finn chewed on his lip. Why did Lydia always make so much sense? But the nagging, gnawing worry that spewed stomach acid and bile like a river of hot lava inside his gut just wouldn't let up.

He looked at Lydia. A woman who had needed him to love her. A love he'd been incapable of giving. 'What if I...?' He could barely even bring himself to say the words. 'What if I don't love him?'

Lydia gave him a sad smile. 'You already do, Finn. Why else are we having this conversation? Just *be* a father. The rest will follow.'

By the time Lydia had ordered him to take a couple of headache pills and have a shower then dragged him to Pete's for brunch, Finn was feeling more human again. She'd nattered away about the weather and her job and the football scores and other inane topics, for which he was grateful, and by midday he was back at his apartment alone, with Lydia's wise words turning over and over in his head.

He wasn't utterly convinced by any of them but he had started to think that being part of his child's life was a responsibility he shouldn't shirk.

How many times as a boy had he vowed to do it different when he became a father? Back in the days before all hope for his future had been quashed. When he'd believed that his life could still be normal.

Lydia was right. A boy needed a father.

A stable, committed presence.

God knew, he and Isaac could have done with one instead of the bunch of losers that had drifted in and out of their mother's life until one had stuck and they'd been pushed out of the nest.

He could do stable and committed.

The light was flashing on the answering-machine from the call earlier and he hit the button to listen to the message.

'Finn…its Evie. I didn't really want to tell this to your machine but…what the hell…it might just be easier all round. I just wanted you to know that I know it's a lot for you to comprehend and I didn't want to tell you to…get something out of you. I'm not after money or any kind of…support. It's okay… you don't have to have anything to do with him…the baby… I just think you deserved to know, that's all. I'm happy to do it all. I'm fine with you never being a part of his life. I don't need that from you. So…that's all really. I just wanted you to know that you're off the hook…if that's what you want. Okay…bye.'

Beep…

Finn stared at the machine. *He was off the hook?* If that's what he wanted?

It should have been what he wanted. He wasn't capable of anything else—he'd just been telling Lydia the same thing. But a surge of anger welled up in his chest, washing over him with all the rage and power of a tsunami.

I'm fine with you never being a part of his life.

You don't have to have anything to do with him.

Like his own father.

Evie was going to raise *his* son by herself. Without his money. His input. His support.

Without him.

It was what he should want. It made sense. She'd love him and nurture him and provide all the things he needed.

Physically and emotionally.

Comfort and security. A real childhood. Aunties, uncles, grandparents. Birthday parties, trips to the beach, photos with Santa.

It should make him happy but it didn't. The anger dissipated quickly, replaced by something that felt very much like…craving. It slid like a serpent through his gut and whispered.

Be a father.

Damn Evie and her independence. Her grand plans. Her *happy to do it all.* Lydia was right—he did have a choice. And he'd be damned if his son would grow up without a father.

Stable and committed trumped absent any day.

An hour later Evie was examining a patient's foot in cubicle two when the curtain snapped back with a harsh screech. She blinked as Finn stood there, glaring at her with his laser gaze, looking all scruffy and shaggy and very, very determined.

'I need to talk to you Dr Lockheart,' he said. 'Now, thank you.'

His imperious tone ticked her off even as her hormones demanded she swoon at his feet in a puddle of lust. Luckily the baby gave her a hefty kick, as if to remind her she had a backbone and to use it.

'I'm busy,' she said, smiling sweetly for the benefit of the elderly lady, who looked startled at his intrusion.

But not as startled as she was!

Finn smiled at the patient as he strode into the cubicle and put his hand under Evie's elbow. 'Important cardiac consult,' he said to the grey-haired woman. 'It won't take a minute.'

'Oh, of course, dear,' the lady said. 'Off you go. Hearts are more important than my silly broken toe.'

Finn smiled at her as he firmed his grip on Evie. 'Let's go,' he said, pulling insistently against her resistance.

Once outside he dropped his hand and stalked down the corridor, naturally assuming she'd just follow him. Evie had a good mind to walk in the opposite direction and force him to come looking for her again but they did need to talk. In fact, she was a little surprised he was willing to do so this early. She'd assumed he'd be thinking about her little bombshell for a while longer.

Which meant he'd probably got her phone message.

So she followed him, glaring at his broad shoulders and the way his hair curled against his collar until both of them disappeared into the on-call room. She steeled herself, taking a moment before she entered. It had taken all her guts to make that phone call this morning when every cell in her body had been urging her to say the opposite.

But she'd meant it. She'd cope if he didn't want a bar of them. *It would hurt, but she'd cope.*

She took a deep breath and pushed through the door. He was standing waiting for her on the opposite side, his arms folded impatiently across his chest.

'You look awful,' she said.

She'd seen Finn in varying states of disarray. Angry, inebriated, in pain, high on pain pills, in denial, unkempt and hungover.

This was about as hungover as she'd ever seen him.

'Trust me, this is an improvement on a few hours ago.'

'Did it help?' she asked, trying to keep the bitterness out of her voice but not really succeeding.

Finn shook his head. 'Nope.'

Evie folded her hands across her chest. 'I left a message on your machine this morning.'

Finn gave a curt nod. 'I got it.'

'Oh.' Evie's hand dropped automatically to her belly, feeling the hard round ball of her expanding uterus. A nurse that morning had joked that she was 'looking preggers' and Evie knew that her baggy scrubs weren't going to help for much longer. 'I mean it, Finn. I don't need you to be part of this.' *I want you to, though, with every fibre of my being.* 'Plenty of kids grow up in single-parent families and they do just fine.'

Finn thought about his own dismal childhood. *Plenty of kids didn't do just fine as well.* And although he'd always thought being a father was the last thing on earth he wanted, he suddenly realised that was wrong.

His child being fatherless was the last thing he wanted.

Didn't *his* son deserve the very, very best? Everything that *he* hadn't had and more? A happy, settled, normal family life? Two people who loved him living and working together to ensure that his life was perfect?

A father. And a mother.

And a puppy!

'I think we should get married,' he said.

Every molecule inside Evie froze for long seconds as his startling sentence filtered through into suddenly sluggish brain cells. 'What?' she asked faintly when she finally found her voice.

Finn wondered if he looked as shocked as she did at the words that had come from nowhere. They hadn't been what he'd been planning to say when he'd practically dragged her into the on-call room but he knew in his bones they were the right words.

His child was growing inside her and, no matter what, he was going to be present. He was going to *be a father*. Conviction and purpose rose in him like an avenging angel.

'You can move in with me. No, wait, I'll buy a house. Somewhere by the harbour, or the northern beaches. Bondi or Coogee. He can join the Nippers or learn to surf.'

Evie's head spun, trying to keep up with Finn's rapid-fire thinking. 'A house?'

'I think kids should grow up near a beach.'

Having been dragged from one hot suburban shoebox to the next, he wanted his son to have the freedom of space and a sea breeze and the rhythm of the ocean in his head when he went to sleep instead of rock music from the bikie neighbours or the blare of the television in the next room.

Finn's thoughts raced in time with his pulse. He was going to *be a father*.

'I'll look into celebrants when I get home.'

Evie stared at him incredulously. He had them married and living at the beach with their surfing son all without a single mention of love.

'We'll do it just after the baby's born. No need to inconvenience ourselves until necessary.'

Evie felt as if she'd entered the twilight zone and waited for eerie music to begin. He didn't even want to get married until the baby had arrived—to inconvenience himself. Could he make it any clearer that this sudden crazy scheme had no basis in human emotion? That it wasn't a love match?

Evie had grown up in a house where her parents had been strangers and she was never, *ever* going to subject herself *or her child* to a cold marriage of convenience.

'No,' she said quietly.

Finn shrugged. 'Well, maybe just before then?'

Evie blinked. Oh, when she was as big as a house and needed to get married in a tent? Was he for real? Did he *not* know how important a wedding was to a woman? Even one who wasn't into sappy ceremonies or big flouncy affairs? Didn't he know that most women wanted declarations of love and commitment when they were proposed to?

If that's what this was…

No, of course he didn't. Because, as with everything in his life, Finn just assumed that she'd jump to do his bidding when he asked.

Wrong.

'I'm not marrying you, Finn.'

Finn dragged his attention back to Evie and her softly spoken rebuttal. He snorted. 'Don't be ridiculous, Evie. This is what you wanted, isn't it?'

More than anything. *But not like this.* 'No. I told you, I can raise this baby without your help.'

Finn shoved a hand on his hip. 'Evie… come on…I know how you feel about me…'

She gave a half-laugh at his gall. 'I always forget how capable you are of breathtaking arrogance. Silly of me, really.'

'Evie,' he sighed, desperate to get on with plans now he'd made up his mind, 'let's not play games.'

Evie felt his impatience rolling off him in waves. 'Okay, fine, let's lay our cards on the table. How do *you* feel about *me*?'

Finn felt the question slug him right between the eyes, which were only just recovering from their brush with the whisky. How he felt about Evie was complicated. But he knew it wasn't what she wanted to hear.

'You want me to tell you that I'm in love with you and we're going to ride off into the sunset and it's all going to be hunky-dory? Because I don't and it isn't. Not in a white-picket-fence way anyway.'

Evie moved to the nearby table and sank into a chair. She'd known he didn't love her but it was still hard to hear.

Finn shut his eyes briefly then opened them and joined her, taking the seat opposite. 'I'm sorry, Evie. It's not you. It's me. There's a lot of…stuff in my life…that's happened. I'm just not capable of loving someone.'

Evie nodded even as the admission tore through all the soft tissue around her heart. Had Isaac's death and the other stuff that Ethan had hinted at really destroyed Finn's ability to love?

'Well, that's what I want,' she said quietly. 'What I need. Love and sunsets and white picket fences. And I won't marry for anything less.'

Finn's lips tightened. This had seemed so easy in theory when the marriage suggestion had slipped from his mouth. She'd say yes and the rest would fall into place. It hadn't occurred to him that Evie would be difficult.

In fact, if anything, he'd counted on those feelings she always wore on her sleeve to work in his favour.

'Not when there's a perfectly good alternative,' she continued. 'I'm happy…really, really happy…that you want to be involved, Finn. But we're going to have to work out a way to co-parent separately because I'm not marrying a man who doesn't love me.'

Her words were quiet but the delivery was deadly and Finn knew that she meant every single one. 'Contrary to what you might think, growing up without two parents kind of sucks, Evie. *Trust me on that.*'

Evie shivered at the bitterness in his words. 'Is that what happened to you?' she murmured. Had Ethan been right about Finn's emotional issues extending further back than Isaac's death?

She watched his face slowly shut down, his eyes become chilly. 'We're not talking about me.'

Evie snorted. 'You tell me to trust you, demand that I marry you, but you clam up when I try to get close? Well *trust me,* Finn, growing up with two parents who hate each other kind of sucks too.'

'At least you had a stable home life,' he snapped.

So he hadn't? 'It wasn't stable,' she said through gritted teeth. 'My father just had enough money to buy the illusion of stability. Ultimately my mother was a drunk who came and went in our lives while my father put nannies in the house and mistresses in his bed.'

Finn's mouth twisted. 'Poor little rich girl.' So Evie's life hadn't been perfect—it had still been a thousand per cent better than his had ever been.

Evie shook her head. He really could be an insensitive jerk when he put his mind to it. 'I won't be with a man who doesn't love me.'

She reiterated each word very carefully.

'You seemed to be with Stuart long enough,' Finn jibed, 'and Blind Freddie could have seen he didn't love you.'

Evie gasped at his cruel taunt, the humiliation from that time revisiting with a vengeance. 'At least he'd pretended to care. I doubt you're even capable of that!'

'You want me to pretend? You want me to lie to you? Okay, fine, Evie I love you. Let's get married.'

She stood, ridiculously close to tears and tired of his haranguing. If he thought this was the way to win her over, he was crazy. 'Go to hell, Finn,' she snapped, and stormed out of the room.

Finn's brain was racing as he took the fire stairs up to his penthouse apartment half an hour later. The lifts were being temperamental again and, frankly, after missing his daily ocean swims he could do with the exercise and the extended thinking time. He was breathing hard by the time he got to the fifth floor and stopped by the landing window to catch his breath and absently admire a large slice of the harbour.

Kirribilli Views apartments had certainly been blessed by the location gods.

The door opened and he turned to find Ava Carmichael entering the fire escape. She looked momentarily surprised and then grinned at him. 'We really must stop meeting like this.'

Finn grunted, remembering their last meeting in this stairwell when he'd come upon Ava crying over her broken marriage. Actually, they'd been through a lot together, with him helping her the day she'd miscarried in the lift and then she and Gladys finding him collapsed from a major infection after his first operation.

Not that they'd ever talked about those things. Ava was like that. For a therapist, she was very non-intrusive. Mostly anyway. There had been an occasion or two where she'd spoken her mind but even then she'd given it to him straight. Hadn't couched anything in vague psychological terms.

He liked that about her.

It was good to know that things had improved for both of them since. He had fully recovered from his injury and she and James had reconciled, having had their first baby just before his second operation and his desertion to *Beach Haven*.

'It's not too late,' Finn said, forcing himself to keep things light. 'We can still make out in the stairwell and no one would know.'

Ava laughed at the rumour she'd threatened to start to blackmail him into seeing her the day after he'd scared the daylights out of all of them with his infection. He'd been in an absolutely foul mood but she'd served him up some home truths anyway.

Not that he'd taken them on board.

He was a stubborn, stubborn man. But she had a soft spot for him because he'd never tried to offer any advice or interfere or make things better when things with James had

been going to hell in a hand basket. Unlike
others. And she'd appreciated that.

'I heard you were back and fully recovered.
Although…' she squinted and inspected his
face a little closer '…you don't look so good
at the moment.'

Finn almost groaned. Did every woman
find it their duty today to tell him he looked
like hell? 'What are you doing here? Didn't
you move to your white-picket-fence house
in the burbs?'

'Just visiting the old stomping ground,' she
said.

Finn turned to look back out the window
and Ava knew she had been dismissed, that
it was her job to walk on down the stairs and
leave him to his obvious brooding, but there
was something achingly lonely about Finn
and they'd been pretty frank with each other
in the past.

Still, she hesitated. She knew that Finn
was an intensely private man. But then Finn
turned his gaze towards her. It was so incredibly turbulent, almost too painful to look at.

'You're a therapist, right?'

Ava laughed. 'I'm a *sex* therapist, Finn.'

He shrugged. 'But you *do* have a psychology degree?'

Ava nodded. 'Is there something you want to talk about?'

Finn shook his head. He wanted to talk to Ava Carmichael about as much as he wanted to become a father but…she'd always given it to him straight and he could do with some insight into the female psyche right now.

'Evie's pregnant. I suggested we get married. She said no. I need her to say yes.'

Ava blinked at the three startling pieces of information. She and Evie were friends, not bosom buddies and they certainly hadn't seen much of each other since her own baby had been born, but she knew more about Finn and Evie's relationship than Finn probably realised.

People told her stuff—it was an occupational hazard.

She knew Evie loved Finn. She knew Finn was a hard man to know and an impossible one to love. She knew that if Evie had turned him down it had been for a pretty good reason.

'Okay…' she wandered closer to him, propping her hip against the window sill. 'So when you say you *suggested*? What did that entail exactly?'

'I said I thought we should get married.'

Ava nodded. 'So, let me guess…you didn't

get down on one knee and do the whole big proposal thing? You kind of…presented it as a fait accompli?' Finn looked away from her probing gaze. 'Am I warm?'

He looked back again, glaring. 'It was more of a…spontaneous thing. Us getting married isn't about any of the hoopla. It's about being practical. About giving our child a normal family with a mother and father living under the same roof. And Evie isn't the kind of woman that goes for all that romantic rubbish.'

Ava arched an eyebrow. 'And how do you know that, Finn? Have you ever really even tried to get to know her?'

He looked away again at the view. 'I know she loves me, Ava. Why be coy about it? Why pretend this isn't what she wants?' He looked back at her. 'This way she gets what she wants and I get what I want.'

'What? A man who doesn't love her?'

Finn wanted to smash the window at her gentle insight. 'Look, Ava…it's complicated. I grew up in a single-parent household and then…' He shook his head. He couldn't tell Ava, no matter what degree she had. He didn't talk about his issues—he just left them behind in the past, where they belonged. Where they couldn't touch him any more. 'I don't want that for my kid.'

Ava pitied him. Finn was a man on the edge and he was the only one who didn't know it. 'Tell *her*, Finn. Not me.'

He shook his head. He was so used to burying it inside he doubted he even knew how to access the words. 'I can't.'

Ava's heart squeezed at the bleakness in his eyes. 'I do recall telling you that this would happen one day, Finn. That by pushing Evie away and not letting her in that one day something would happen and you'd find yourself locked out of Evie's life.'

Finn nodded miserably. She'd said exactly that. Yelled it at him, actually, when he was being rude and stubborn and difficult, refusing to see Evie after he'd been hospitalised with the infection.

'Seriously?' he said. 'You're going with an *I told you so* now? Where'd you get that degree?' he grouched. 'In a cornflakes packet?'

Ava smiled. 'Coco Pops, actually.'

Finn gave a half-smile before turning back to the window. 'Fine. How do I fix it?'

'Maybe it's time to stop pushing her away. To open yourself up.'

Finn pressed his forehead against the glass. She may as well have told him to stand in the middle of the hospital naked. 'What? No pill?'

Ava shook her head. 'I'm afraid not.'

'You're a lousy therapist,' he muttered.

She laughed. 'What do you expect for free?'

CHAPTER SIX

A MONTH PASSED and it was business as usual at Sydney Harbour Hospital. Finn was back on board, being his brilliant, arrogant, grouchy self. Anyone who'd thought that with him now fully recovered from his injury his mood might have improved had been sorely mistaken. Evie's recalcitrance had taken over from the pain and restrictions that had made him notoriously moody, resulting in a crankier than ever Dr Kennedy.

But given that Prince Khalid's cheque had made the hospital one million dollars richer, no one was about to call him on it. Those on his team just knew—you did your job with skill and competence and stayed the hell out of Finn's way.

Even Finn and Evie's relationship had gone back to that of polite detachment, which was causing an absolute buzz on the grapevine. At twenty-five weeks Evie could no longer hide her pregnancy and with everyone knowing Finn was the baby-daddy, speculation was rife.

Were they together?

Would they get married?

Were they already married and keeping it a secret?

Why couldn't they barely say two words to each other?

Did they even like each other?

Everything from the hows and wheres of the baby's conception to a potential wedding and the custody arrangements were red-hot topics.

Everything about Finn and Evie were red-hot topics—like they were freaking royalty.

The fact that both of them were tight-lipped with answers to any of the questions being asked didn't help.

And in the absence of truth there was gossip.

Evie soldiered on regardless of the whispers. Finn stayed away and she alternated between being mad and glad. But mostly she just wished she knew what the hell was going on inside his head and where they went from here. Sooner or later they were going to need to talk but she was damned if she was going to instigate it.

As far as she was concerned, the ball was firmly in his court!

Evie was late arriving at Pete's—the pub that had stood across the road from the hospital for twenty years—on Saturday afternoon. Bella and Lexi were already seated and deep in conversation.

Pete smiled at her from behind the bar and mouthed, 'The usual?' at her. She nodded, the usual these days being sparkling water instead of a nice cold bottle of beer.

Not that abstaining from drinking for nine months was a hardship but she did miss it occasionally after a long day on her feet—and it had been a very hectic day.

She joined her sisters, pushing into the cubicle next to Bella to give Lexi some room. Two pregnant women on one side of a booth was one pregnant woman too many, especially given Lexi's about-to-pop status.

'How's it going?' Evie asked her sister as Pete brought her water over in a wine glass. Bless him, at least she had the illusion she was drinking something fortified.

Lexi grimaced. 'This baby is sitting so low

I feel like my uterus is going to fall out every time I stand up.'

Evie and Bella laughed. They both knew that Lexi and Sam, a transplant surgeon, were ecstatic about the fast-approaching due date. Their relationship was stronger than ever now after their years apart. 'Pretty sure that's not possible,' Evie said.

Lexi laughed too. 'There's always a first time.'

They chatted for a while about baby things, both of her sisters being careful to avoid the F word even though she could tell they were dying to ask her about the latest with Finn. But what was there to say? There was no latest.

The baby kicked and Evie grimaced.

'What is it?' Bella asked. 'Did he kick?' Evie nodded, her hand smoothing over the spot where the baby was busy boogying. 'Can I feel?' Bella asked, her hands automatically gliding over Evie's belly to where her hand was, exclaiming in awe when the baby performed right on cue.

Evie noticed the wistful look on her younger sister's face as she enjoyed the show. 'I'm sorry, Bells, this must be hard for you.'

Bella had cystic fibrosis and Sam had performed a double lung transplant on her less than a year ago. She and Charlie, an ortho-pod the hospital, desperately wanted a baby but there were risks that neither of them was willing to take on Bella's health, not to mention the sceptre of any baby also having CF.

'It's fine. I'm just pleased neither of you carry the gene so my lovely little niece and nephew will be fine.'

She smiled at them both but Evie could tell it took a huge effort. Poor Bella had already had so much taken from her in life.

'Besides,' Bella continued, 'I get to be the cool aunty, who fills them up with lollies and ice cream and lets them watch scary movies till midnight and teaches them to drive.'

'And designs fabulous couture for their proms and weddings from your latest collection,' Lexi added.

'That right,' Bella agreed. Her new lungs had given her more freedom to make her fashion design dream a reality. 'And you can organise fabulous parties for them,' Bella said.

Lexi, an events planner, grinned. 'Starting with your baby shower,' she said to Evie.

Evie laughed. 'Steady on, there's plenty of time to be worrying about that. Just you concentrate on getting this little one…' she patted Lexi's belly '…out. We'll worry about my baby shower a few months down the track.'

Lexi shifted uncomfortably. 'Deal.'

'So, Bells,' Evie said, as Pete plonked another wine glass of sparkling water in front of her, 'tell us about your course. What are you working on?'

They nattered away for the next hour and Evie felt lighter and happier than she had in weeks. Between Finn, the gossip and the baby, she'd had a lot on her mind. It was fabulous to leave that all beyond for a while and be pulled headlong into girly, sister stuff.

Or at least it was until Finn showed up in jeans and a T-shirt, looking all rugged and stubbly and very determined. She'd seen that look before and went on instant alert despite the flutter in the region of her heart.

'Evie,' he greeted her, with a quick nod of his head to Lexi and Bella.

Evie frowned at him. 'Is there something wrong?'

He shook his head. 'I have something I'd like to show you. If your sisters can spare you…of course.'

Finn's face ached from being polite when all he really wanted to do was snatch her up and throw her over his shoulder. The refined, educated side of him was horrified by the prehistoric notion but the rampaging Neanderthal he'd become since she'd turned him down quite frankly didn't give a damn at the spectacle that would ensue should he follow through on his impulse.

'Finn…' Evie sighed. She didn't have the energy to fight today.

'Please, Evie.'

Evie blinked. Finn wasn't one for saying 'please'. Not even when he'd *suggested* they get married had he thrown in a 'please'.

'Where exactly are you taking her?' Bella asked, placing a protective hand on her sister's arm.

Bella didn't like the way he'd been treating Evie, especially his silence this last month. If she were pregnant there was no way Charlie would treat her so abysmally. He'd wrap in her cotton wool, which was no less than any woman deserved. Especially Evie, who'd been the Lockheart family rock for ever and worked such long, punishing hours.

'It's a surprise,' Finn hedged.

'Is it a good surprise?' Bella demanded. 'Will she like it, Finn Kennedy, because I don't care how much money you bring into the hospital's coffers or how brilliant everyone says you are, frankly I think you can be pretty damn obtuse.'

'Bella,' Lexi said reproachfully.

But Finn gave a grudging smile. Trust another Lockheart to tell him like it was. Bella had been pretty easy to dismiss due to being sickly most of her life but those new lungs had certainly given her a whole lot of breath! 'Yes,' he conceded, 'it's a good surprise.'

Evie's pulse fluttered at her wrist and tap-danced at her temple as Bella removed her hand. He didn't look any softer but his words were encouraging. Maybe they were going to have an adult conversation about the way forward?

'Fine,' she said, dropping a kiss on Bella's cheek before she eased herself out of the booth. Finn stepped aside for her and Evie was excruciatingly aware of the sudden rabid interest—some subtle, some not so subtle—directed towards them as she gave Lexi a quick peck.

She turned to Finn, ignoring the speculation she could practically feel coursing through Pete's like an electrical current. 'Lead on,' she said.

She breathed a little easier once they'd got out of the pub and were walking to his car, parked at the kerb outside. It was black and low with only two seats—the ultimate status symbol—and it surprised her. She'd never seen Finn's car. He walked to work as everyone who lived at Kirribilli Views did, and like everyone else at his professional level and with his abrasive personality didn't have a social life that really required one.

She supposed the women he'd dated probably thought it was hot and cool. Good-looking doctor—check! Racy car—check! But all she could think as the engine purred to life was, *Where was he going to put the baby seat?*

'So what's the big surprise?' she asked as Finn negotiated the late-afternoon traffic.

'Patience,' he said, his eyes not leaving the road. 'Patience.'

So they didn't talk for the fifteen minutes it took to get where they were going. Evie looked around bewildered as they pulled up at a house in Lavender Bay, not far from the hospital or the harbour. In fact, as she climbed out of his car—something that would probably be impossible at nine months—she could see down to the harbour where the early evening light had laid its gentle fingers and across the other side to the tall distinctive towers of the SHH and further on to the large garish clown mouth of Luna Park and the famous bridge that spanned the harbour.

A breeze that smelled of salt and sand

picked up her hair, blowing a strand across her face as she tracked the path of a yellow and green ferry. She pulled it away as she turned to face Finn, who was opening the low gate of the house where they were parked.

'Okay, so…what are we doing here?'

'All will be revealed shortly,' he said as he gestured for her to follow him up the crumbling cement path.

Evie frowned. Whose place was this? Did he want her to meet someone? Someone who might help her understand him? A patient? A relative? Lydia? However she fitted into the puzzle that was Finn. His mother? His grandmother? *Did he even have either of those?* He never spoke of them.

It had to be someone he knew, though, because he had a key and as she watched him walk up the three stairs and traverse the old-fashioned balcony covered by a Seventies-style awning he didn't even bother with knocking. Just slipped the key into the lock and pushed the door open.

He turned to her. 'Come,' he said as he stepped into the house.

Evie rolled her eyes. The man was clueless. Utterly clueless. But she followed him anyway because she was dying to know who lived in this gorgeous little cottage overlooking the harbour and what they had to do with Finn.

Maybe it was a clue to his life that he always kept hidden from her. From everyone.

She stepped inside, her heels clacking against smooth polished floorboards the colour of honey. The sound echoed around the empty house. The rooms, as she moved through, following Finn, were devoid of furniture, curtains or blinds and floor coverings. Soaring ceilings graced with decorative roses added to the cavernous echo.

He opened the back door and she followed him down the three stairs to the back entertaining area and then onto a small patch of grass, the back fence discreetly covered by a thick row of established shrubbery.

'Well?' he said, turning around with his arms splayed wide like a game-show host. 'It's beautiful, don't you think?'

He was smiling at her, a rare smile that went all the way to his eyes, lighting them up like a New Year's Eve laser display, and Evie's foolish heart skipped a beat. 'Yes,' she said hesitantly, smiling back.

'It's yours,' he said. 'Ours. I bought it. As a wedding gift. The perfect place to raise our son.'

Evie stared at him for the longest time as

everything around her seemed to slow right down to a snail's pace. The flow of blood in her veins, the passage of air in her lungs, the distant blare of a ferry horn on the harbour. Then the slow death of her smile as realisation dawned.

'Is this another way of *suggesting* we get married?' she asked, her quiet voice sounding loud in the silence that seemed to have descended on the back yard.

Finn shook his head vigorously. 'Absolutely not. It's a proposal. I was wrong last time just…assuming. I should have asked you. I got the call this afternoon from the real estate agent that she was mine.'

Ours, she corrected silently knowing that the gesture, while grand, was empty. It was obvious he didn't think of it as theirs. That it was just another way of getting what he wanted.

He reached out and took her hand. 'What do you say, Evie? Let's get married. Let's raise our son together, here in this house with the harbour just there and everything he could ever want.'

Evie looked into his gorgeously shaggy, earnest face. A part of her whispered, *Do it.* Say yes. Take the fake marriage. Take whatever he's offering. You can make him love you with time and patience.

And it was, oh, so tempting.

But she couldn't. She just couldn't.

She wanted more than that. She wanted it all—the whole hearts and flowers catastrophe. If she'd learned anything from her own parents' marriage and years of navigating a fraught household, it was that you couldn't make someone love you if they didn't.

No matter how hard you tried.

And you had to start as you meant to go on.

She withdrew her hand from his. 'No.'

She refused to live on Finn's crumbs as her mother had on her father's. If they were going to enter into a marriage then she wanted all of him.

'Hell, Evie,' Finn said, shaking his head incredulously. 'I bought you a house. What more do you want from me?'

'I can buy my own house,' she snapped.

'Then what *do* you want' he demanded.

'You, Finn,' she yelled. 'I want you. I want you to open up to me. To know every secret, every ugly thought, every tear you've ever shed. I want to know about every sad, sorry day of your existence. And I want you to *want* to know about *mine*. I want to know about Isaac and the day that he died in your arms and about who the hell Lydia is and how she fits into your life and about your childhood and your time in the army as a trauma surgeon.'

Evie was breathing hard as she finished and she'd just scraped the surface of the things she wanted to know about the man she loved. 'That's what I want,' she said, ramming her hands onto her hips, pulling her shirt taut across her bump. 'Anything less is asking me to debase myself. And I deserve better than that.'

Finn reeled from her list. *She wanted too much.* She wanted stuff he'd never given to anyone. Not to Lydia. Not even to Isaac.

Finn steeled himself to be the practical one. Obviously the pregnancy was making levelheaded Evie a trace emotional.

'None of those things are open to negotiation,' he said, his voice steely. 'Neither are they required to make a life together. I'm sure if we're both practical we can make it work, Evie.'

Evie's temper flared at his condescension. He truly thought he could just wear her down. She'd swallowed a lot of pride where Finn was concerned because she loved him and she'd known he'd been hurting and she'd seen the injured soul under the gruff and bluff but she drew the line here. She would not become his wife—give him her all—and end up married to a stranger.

'Okay, then,' she snapped. 'Tell me how it will work, Finn. How? We get married and have a committed normal relationship where you take out the rubbish and I hang out the washing and we argue over the TV remote and snuggle in bed on the weekends with the newspapers?'

She glared at him as she drew breath. 'Or is it just a name-only thing? Do we sleep in the same bed to keep up the ruse for our son? Or apart? Do we have some kind of open marriage where we discreetly see other people? Or do we just go without sex for the next twenty-ish years and you spend a lot of time in the shower and I run up an account at the sex shop we just passed?'

Finn blinked at her vehemence, lost for words, but she seemed to have paused for a moment and was looking at him like it was his turn to add to the conversation. 'I haven't really thought about the nitty-gritty, Evie.'

'*Bum-bah*!' she snorted. 'Wrong answer. Try again. You want me to accept this proposal?' She folded her arms. 'Convince me.'

Finn picked carefully through words and phrases in his head, hoping that he found the right ones to convince her. 'I assumed we'd be sharing the same bed. In the…' he searched around for a delicate way to put it '…fullest sense of the word.'

'Well, I just bet you did, didn't you? Works well for you, doesn't it, to have sex on tap. No need for all those showers then.'

Finn wondered if Evie was maybe becoming a little hysterical but he was damned if he was going to be made out to be the bad guy here because he wanted to have sex with his wife. 'No need for you to take out shares in sex-toy companies either,' he pointed out, his jaw aching from trying to stay rational.

'Well, I wouldn't count on that.'

It was Finn's turn to snort. 'You know well enough, Evie Lockheart, that I can make you come loud enough to scare nesting birds on the other side of the harbour.'

She shrugged. 'So can a little imagination.'

He quirked an eyebrow. 'It can't hold you afterwards.'

'Maybe not. But at least it's not going to break my heart a little more each time and slowly erode my self-respect.'

'Damn it, Evie,' he fumed as his control started to slip. *'This is not what I wanted.* I didn't want to be a father but it's happening and I'm here. Do you think you could at least meet me halfway?'

Evie grappled with her escalating temper. He was right. He was here. Even if he was being a total idiot about it. She took a calm, steadying breath.

'*This*,' she said, repeating his open-armed action from earlier as she indicated the house and yard, 'isn't halfway, Finn. *This* is full throttle. Halfway is agreeing to a parenting schedule. Talking about how it's going to affect our jobs and what we can do to lessen the impact on two households. It's talking about what schools he should go to and getting our wills in order.'

Finn shook his head. She seemed much calmer now but he could feel it all slipping away. This was not how he'd planned today would go. 'What about the house?' he demanded.

'It's fabulous,' she said gently. God knew, she'd move in tomorrow if things were different between them. 'And our son is going to love being here with you. But I'm not going to marry you, Finn. Not when you don't love me.'

'I don't want some modern rubbish arrangement for my kid,' he said stubbornly. He didn't want his son to be bouncing between houses—his whole childhood had been like that and he'd hated it. 'It'll be confusing for him.'

'He won't have known anything else,' she murmured, and then she shook her head. 'It's funny, I never picked you as a traditionalist.'

'Kids should be raised by their parents. Together.'

'Sure. In an ideal world. But what we've got here isn't ideal, is it, Finn? And I'm pretty sure I'm capable of doing my bit to raise our son.'

Her calmness was getting on his nerves. He knew for sure he wasn't capable of raising a child by himself. He needed her. He needed her to provide the love and comfort stuff. The nurturing. He could teach him to build a fire and climb a tree and how to fish. He needed Evie there to make up for the stuff he wasn't capable of in all the quiet, in-between times.

'Well, you haven't exactly done such a stellar job so far,' he lashed out. 'You've got yourself electrocuted, almost drowned and followed that up by a case of hypothermia.'

Evie gasped, her hand automatically going to her belly, as if to shield the baby from the insult. If she'd been a more demonstrative woman, she might just have slapped him. 'The baby is perfectly fit and healthy and completely unharmed,' she said, her voice vibrating with hurt.

His gaze dropped to where her hand cradled her belly and he felt the irrational surge of anger from the day she'd been caught up in the rip break over him again. 'Well, that was sheer luck, wasn't it?' he snapped.

Evie wanted to scream and rant and stomp her foot but it was useless and exhausting and getting them nowhere. Finn was being his usual pig-headed self and she should know better than to try and reason with him in this mood.

She shook her head at him, swallowing down all the rage and fury and sucking up his bad temper like she always did. The only thing she had was the high ground. And now seemed like a very good time to take it.

'Goodbye, Finn,' she said, turning on her heel and marching through the house.

He followed her, calling out to her about being reasonable and driving her back, but a taxi came along just as she was opening the gate and it pulled in when she waved, and she didn't look back as Finn told her to stop being ridiculous. She just opened the door and told the driver to go, go, go.

A week later Evie was lying in bed on her day off after five day shifts, too exhausted to get up to relieve her full bladder, which the baby was taking great delight in using as a trampoline. She hadn't heard boo from Finn all week. In fact, she'd only glimpsed him once, and she didn't know whether that had been his passive-aggressive way of agreeing to do it her way or if he was just off plotting his next grand gesture.

She suspected the latter, although right now she was too tired to care.

Another five minutes of baby gymnastics and she could ignore the need to go no longer. She rolled out of bed and did her business. She was heading back again when there was a knock on her door. She wistfully eyed the corner of her bed, which she could see through the open door.

It was probably just Bella, who had taken to dropping in all the time to check on her. She could probably just ignore it but the knock came again and she didn't have the heart to leave her sister on the doorstep.

Except it wasn't Bella when she opened the door. It was Lydia.

Evie blinked, feeling like an Amazon next to the tiny redhead. She tried to suck in her belly but that was no longer possible. 'Oh… Hi…Lydia?'

Lydia smiled at her as she checked out

Evie's belly. 'Well, he's right,' she said. 'You're definitely pregnant.'

'Er...yes,' Evie said, struck by how truly bizarre this moment was. Not knowing Lydia's exact relationship with Finn made this meeting kind of awkward. For her anyway. Lydia didn't seem ready to scratch her eyes out—in fact, she seemed friendly—so maybe they didn't have that kind of history?

'Do you think I could come in?' Lydia asked. 'I've come on behalf of Finn.'

Evie groaned—Finn had sent an emissary? She was too tired for this. 'Look, Lydia, if Finn's sent you to offer me some crazy incentive—money or diamonds or the goose that lays the golden eggs—I really need to let you know right off the bat that you're wasting your breath.'

Lydia pursed her lips. 'Oh, dear...the house,' she tutted. 'It's worse than I thought.'

Evie frowned. 'Huh?'

'Can I, please, just come in and explain?' Evie hesitated and Lydia dived in to reassure her. 'I've come on behalf of Finn but he doesn't know I'm here. *He'd be furious if he did.* But I haven't seen him this...bleak in a very long time and I can't bear it any longer.'

Evie could hear the woman's genuine concern and worry as she had that day Lydia had told her Finn's whereabouts. She got the sense that Lydia loved Finn and the spike of jealousy that drove into her chest almost knocked Evie flat. She reached for the door to steady herself, the overwhelming urge to slam it in Lydia's face warring with her curiosity.

Curiosity won out.

Part of Evie needed to know where Lydia fitted into Finn's life.

Evie fell back and ushered her inside. She played the perfect hostess, fixing Lydia a cup of coffee and some green tea for herself. They sat on opposite sides of the coffee table, sipping at their drinks for a moment or two, and then Evie voiced what she'd sensed from the beginning.

'You love him?'

Lydia nodded. 'Yes.'

Evie gripped the cup at the other woman's calm response, her pulse pounding in her ears. What must Lydia think of her? Carrying Finn's baby. Did Finn love her back? Was that why he couldn't love her?

'I'm sorry, I didn't know…' She put a hand on her belly. 'I would never have…if I had known he was with you.'

Lydia frowned. 'What?' She made an annoyed little noise at the back of her throat. 'He hasn't told you about me, has he?' She reached across the coffee table and patted Evie's hand. 'Finn's my brother-in-law. I'm Isaac's wife. Widow, to be precise.'

Evie felt a rush of relief like a slug of Finn's whisky to her system. She let out a pent-up breath in a loud rush. 'His sister-in-law?'

Lydia grinned again. 'Yes.'

'Oh,' Evie said, lost for words as the high robbed her of her ability to form a complex sentence. 'That's good.' She smiled. 'That's good.'

Lydia nodded. 'Although in the interests of full disclosure we did have a…relationship. A very messed-up one for a few years after Isaac's death. I was a complete wreck…it was a very dark time… I think we both held on for much longer than we should have because we were each other's link to Isaac.'

'Oh,' Evie said again, still having trouble with sentences but this time because of Lydia's frankness. Finn and Isaac's widow had been lovers? 'Did he…did he love you?'

Lydia shook her head. 'Not in that way, no. I wanted him to…needed him to at the time… but he's been through a lot…seen a lot…he's a complex man. He doesn't love easily.'

Evie nodded slowly. 'Tell me about it.'

'You love him?'

'Yes.'

'And yet you won't marry him.' Lydia smiled. 'You have him quite riled up.'

Evie shrugged, looking into the bottom of her cup. 'He doesn't love me. And I'm not settling for anything less.'

'Good for you.' Lydia laughed. 'If it's any consolation, though, I think he does love you.'

She looked up at Lydia sharply, expecting to find her looking as flippant as the remark, but she seemed deadly serious. 'Well, I think he does too,' she said. 'But he has to say it. He has to admit it. To himself more than anything.'

Lydia nodded. 'Yes. For a man so bloody intelligent he can be exceedingly dim-witted.'

Evie laughed and Lydia joined her. When their laughter died Lydia suddenly sat forward and grabbed Evie's hand. 'Don't give up on him, Evie, please. He needs you.'

Evie was reminded of Ethan's words. It spoke volumes that Finn had people who loved and cared about him.

'I need him too,' she said. 'But I need all of him.'

Lydia let her hand go. 'Of course you do.' She sipped at her coffee. 'He showed me the house,' she said after a while.

'Ah,' Evie murmured. 'The house.'

'You don't like the house?' Lydia asked, her brow crinkling.

'I freaking love the house,' Evie muttered. 'But I don't want grand gestures from him.'

Lydia gave her a sad smile. 'You have to understand what that house means to Finn.'

'Oh, yes?' Evie asked, trying to keep the jealousy out of her voice. 'And what's that? Believe me, I'd love to know. But he doesn't tell me anything. He just wants to install me there like bloody Miss Haversham.'

Lydia pursed her lips again as if deciding what to say next. Evie hoped and prayed she'd say something, anything, that would give her some insight into the man she loved.

'Finn and Isaac grew up in the system,' Lydia said. 'Their mother abandoned them when Finn was eight. Isaac was six. It was… tough. They got passed around a lot. Finn fought to keep them together, which was hard when most families only wanted one troubled child and that was usually the much sunnier Isaac. There was a lot of rejection. A lot of…bouncing around. Finn would tell Isaac stories about their dad coming to take them away to Luna Park for the day and a ride on a ferry then bringing them back to his home by the sea.'

Evie sat for long moments, letting the

import of Lydia's words sink in. Finn had bought his childhood fantasy home for his own son, the house he'd never known, with the hope of providing his child with an up-bringing he'd never had.

She sat very still, moved almost to tears. And yet she was blindingly jealous too. Why had she had to hear this story from Lydia? Why couldn't he have told her himself? If he'd told her this the day he'd taken her to the house she might not have been so bloody angry all week.

'He told you all this?' she asked, looking up at Lydia.

Lydia shook her head with a wry smile. 'Good grief, no. Isaac did. Finn never speaks of it. I doubt he's ever told anyone.'

It shouldn't have made her feel better. The story was tragic and awful. But somehow it did. Somehow knowing that he hadn't told any woman about his younger years gave her hope. Hope that he would open up to her about it eventually.

Over time.

Which was what they had now. Time. Before the baby was born.

Maybe she could use it wisely to get them what they both wanted?

CHAPTER SEVEN

Ava had been in her office for one minute on Monday morning when the door opened and Finn stormed in.

'What do women want?' he demanded.

Ava looked up from the mail she'd been opening. He was in his usual work attire of a carelessly worn suit, his tie pulled askew. 'And good morning to you too, Finn.'

Finn waved his hand dismissively. 'I bought her a house—*a goddamn house*—and she still turned me down.'

'You bought her a house because…you love her?'

He shoved his hand on his hip. 'This has nothing to do with love. I bought her a house so our son has a roof over his head.'

'Right…so you bought her a house but you don't love her? Goodness.' Ava tsked. 'That's a tad ungrateful.'

Finn glared at her. 'There's no need for sarcasm.'

Ava sighed as Finn prowled back and forth in front of her desk. 'Okay. Did she say why she turned you down?'

Finn stopped pacing. 'She said she could buy her own house.' He shot her an incredulous look. 'Like I'd offended her feminist principles.'

Ava nodded patiently. Of course Evie Lockheart could buy her own house. With or without the Lockheart fortune behind her. But years of being a psychologist told her there was a lot more to Evie's refusal than an affront to feminism.

'What else?'

'What?'

'Did she say anything else?'

Finn took up prowling again and Ava leaned back in her chair to wait him out.

'She wants me to *open up to her*,' he said eventually.

Ava suppressed a smile. Opening up was not something that Finn was known for. He made it sound as if Evie had asked for a sparkly unicorn or some other such nonsense.

'And you don't want to do that?'

'How does talking about my past have anything to do with raising our son together?' he demanded.

Ava swung slightly in her chair, watching Finn pace. 'Because it's what couples do?' she suggested.

'We're not a couple,' he snapped, coming to an abrupt halt.

She quirked an eyebrow. 'And yet you want her to marry you…?'

'None of that stuff is important to a successful future together.'

Ava knew he was dead wrong and she suspected that somewhere beneath all the injury and barriers he knew it too. But it wasn't her job to tell him he was wrong. 'Is it important what *you* think or what *she* needs?'

He glared at her. 'Goddamn it. Can't you just give me one piece of useful advice instead of answering every question with another question? You're a sex therapist, aren't you supposed to be full of practical ideas about making relationships work?'

Ava sighed. He was far from ready for practical exercises and she should be annoyed that he wanted her to give him a magic wand without doing any of the hard yards he obviously needed. But this was Finn, who wasn't a client, and for Evie's sake maybe she could help.

'Fine.' She folded her arms across her chest. 'Woo her, Finn.'

He frowned. 'Woo her? Are we living in Shakespearian England all of a sudden?' he scoffed.

Ava knew that good wooing took time and if Evie was smart she'd use it to her advantage. 'You wanted my advice.' She shrugged. 'You got it.'

'I've already got her pregnant—don't you think it's a little late for the wooing?'

Ava shook her head. 'It's never too late for wooing.'

Finn shut his eyes. *Bloody hell*. He'd bought her a house and now he was going to have to *woo* her as well?

He opened his eyes. 'Gee, thanks.'

Ava grinned at Finn's look of distaste. 'Don't mention it.'

Finn knocked on Evie's door that night in his suit, juggling some flowers and a bag of Indian takeaway. He knew she was on days off because he'd checked the emergency department's medical roster at lunchtime.

He'd been brooding about Ava's advice all day and by the time he'd finished his afternoon theatre list he'd decided it might be a worth a try. He had time, after all, and instead of rushing like a bull at a gate, which was what he had been doing, maybe a little subtlety *was* called for.

But it had better show dividends pretty quickly because, come hell or high water, they would be married by the time the baby was born.

The door opened and he suddenly felt awkward and unsure of himself standing there with flowers. Women usually came to him—flowers and that kind of thing weren't his style.

Evie blinked. 'Finn?'

'I have flowers,' he said, pushing them into her arms. He lifted up the plastic bag in his other hand. 'And Indian takeaway. Have you eaten?'

Evie shook her head, the aroma of yellow roses and oriental lilies enveloping her. 'I was just doing some…yoga.'

Finn noted her workout gear. Skin-tight Lycra knee-length leggings. An equally form-fitting top with a round neckline and spaghetti straps that bared her shoulders and stretched over her full breasts and rounded belly. Her hair had been scraped back into a messy ponytail.

'I see,' he said, exceedingly self-conscious

as he tried not to stare. She seemed to get bigger every time he saw her.

'Come in,' she said, falling back to allow him entry.

Finn stepped inside and then followed her through to the lounge room. There was some low Gregorian chant playing from a sound system somewhere and he noted the yoga mat on the floor. He sat where she indicated on the three-seater lounge and started to pull the containers out while she took the flowers out of sight.

He heard water running, a fridge door opening then shuffling of crockery and tinkling of glasses as he pulled the lids off. He almost called out to just bring some cutlery but he supposed part of the wooing process was to eat off good plates rather than straight from the containers.

Evie, her brain busy trying to fathom what Finn was up to now, was back in the lounge room in a couple of minutes, balancing a tray and the vase of flowers. Finn, who'd taken off his jacket and tie, stood and relieved her of the tray as she placed the vase on top of the television cabinet and used a remote to turn the music off. When she turned back he'd unloaded the tray and her plate was waiting for her, the napkin a bright slash of red against the snowy white pattern.

He was pouring them both sparkling water and he smiled at her as he handed her the glass. A smile that went straight to her insides. She sat towards the end of the lounge, tucking a foot up underneath her, being careful to leave a cushion's distance between them as he asked her what she wanted then proceeded to plate it up for her, passing it and the napkin over when he was done.

She took it and sat unmoving for a few moments as he turned his attention to his own meal. When that was done he smiled at her again and then tucked in.

'Okay,' she said, placing her plate on the coffee table. 'What's going on?'

Finn, in mid-swallow, thought about feigning obtuseness as Bella had already accused him of being obtuse anyway. But he was a cards-on-the-table kind of guy.

He finished his mouthful and took a drink of water as the spicy lamb korma heated his mouth. 'Ava thinks I should woo you.'

Evie frowned. 'Ava? *Ava Carmichael?*'

Finn nodded. 'The one and only.'

'You're seeing Ava?'

'Yes. No. Not like that. We just…chat sometimes…'

Evie was lost for words. 'I…see…' What on earth could she say to such a startling revelation?

It was Finn's turn to frown. 'You don't like it.' He shook his head. 'I knew it was a dumb idea,' he muttered.

Evie shook her head. 'No, I just…' Just what? Was shocked, amazed, flabbergasted? That Finn Kennedy had not only asked a sex therapist for advice about their relationship but had also obviously taken it on board. 'It's sweet…really sweet,' she ended lamely.

'Great,' Finn grumbled, as he also put his plate down. 'Why don't you just pat me on the head and tell me to run along?'

Evie watched as he ran a hand through his hair. This was her chance to start making inroads into his reserve. If he'd finally dropped his bullying tactics and was willing to take others' advice he might just be open to doing things her way.

She leaned forward, resting her bent elbows on her knees. 'I don't want you to woo me, Finn.'

Finn gave a self-deprecating smile. 'Probably just as well. I obviously suck at it.'

Evie laughed. 'You were doing fine. I'm sure with a little practice you'll be perfect.'

He glanced at her. 'But it's not what you want?'

She shook her head slowly. 'How about I do you a deal? I *will* marry you *after* the baby is born if we spend these next few months getting to know each other first.'

Finn's heart started to pound in his chest. It was the same thing she'd told him she wanted at the house. Except she'd made a major concession—she was promising to marry him. 'You've changed your tune,' he said warily.

Evie nodded. 'I spoke to Lydia. She thinks you're worth a little perseverance.'

Finn felt every muscle in his body tense. 'Lydia?'

Evie almost shivered at the sudden drop in his tone. 'She told me a little about you and Isaac growing up in the care system and what the house at Lavender Bay symbolises for you. She asked me not to give up on you. So, by the way, did Ethan.'

Finn wanted to roar at the interference. How dared they talk about him behind his back? This stuff was deeply, deeply personal! 'Lydia *and Ethan*,' he ground out, 'should really learn to keep their big mouths shut.'

'They care about you, Finn,' she murmured. 'As I do. And I'm willing to meet you at this halfway you wanted, to marry you, but only if you're willing to meet me halfway. I want us to get to know each other, Finn. No holds barred. No topic off limits.'

Finn felt the slow burn of anger being doused by hope as the push and pull of emotions seesawed inside him.

He could have what he wanted.

But at what cost?

Was she hoping her amateur attempts at psychology would result in some breakthrough? 'Do you think me spilling my guts to you will make me love you somehow? Is that what you're hoping for, Evie? Because it's probably just going to make me resent you.'

Goose-bumps broke out on Evie's arms at the conviction in his voice. She shrugged. 'Well, I guess that's a risk I'm prepared to take. This isn't about making you love me, Finn.'

'Isn't it? Isn't it?' he demanded, his emotions swinging again. 'So when we get to the end of it all and you know all the sordid details of my life, especially the bit where I don't know how to love anybody because I grew up without any and I still can't give you the love you want, you're still going to marry me? Is that right?'

Evie swallowed at the stark facts he hadn't

bothered to sugar-coat. 'Yes. That's right. I just want to know you better. Is it so wrong to want to know the man you're married to? The father of your child?'

Finn hated that she was so bloody rational. They were talking about his life and there was nothing rational about that. He stood and glared down at her. 'So you want to know how it felt to have Isaac die in my arms?' he demanded. 'And my awful childhood with a mother who abandoned us? You want to know all my dirty little secrets?'

Evie nodded, knowing it was vital to stay calm in the face of his consternation. She understood she was asking a *very big thing* of him. It was only fair for him to rail against it for a while.

'Yes,' she said quietly. 'I don't want you to tell me everything in one night. We can build up to the hard stuff but…yes, I want to know it all.'

Finn felt lost as the storm raged inside him. He'd thought she'd back down in the face of his outrage but she wasn't even blinking. He felt angry and scared and panicked as he contemplated what she wanted.

Cornered.

And then Evie slipped her hand into his and it was like the storm suddenly calmed and he had an overwhelming urge to tell her everything. Completely unburden himself. 'Sit down,' she said. 'Eat your curry. It's getting cold.'

Finn sat, his heart beating like a bongo drum as he raked his hands through his hair. She picked up his plate and handed it to him and he took it, eating automatically as his thoughts whizzed around and collided with each other like atoms on speed.

'What do you want to know?' he asked eventually after half his meal had been demolished and he couldn't stand the silence any longer.

'It's okay,' Evie said. 'We don't have to talk tonight. Just...tell me about your day.'

He frowned. 'My day?'

Evie gave a half-laugh at his bewildered expression. 'Yes. Your day. You know, the stuff married people talk about all the time.'

It was awkward at first but they were soon chatting about safe hospital topics—his theatre list tomorrow, how Prince Khalid was going, some new whizz-bang monitor he wanted for the cath lab and the new salads on the canteen menu. And before Evie knew it, two hours had passed and Finn was on his second cup of coffee.

Even he looked surprised when he checked

his watch as he drained the dregs from his mug. 'I guess I'd better get going,' he said, looking at her, curiously not wanting to leave.

Evie nodded. It would be the easiest thing in the world to ask him to stay. He'd actually been acting like a human being for once and he looked tired and stubbly and masculine and it had been so long that she wanted to reach across the gap and sink into his arms. But she didn't want to mess with what she was trying to establish now.

Sex would just distract them.

Suddenly the baby gave a swift kick that stole her breath and she gasped involuntarily and soothed her hand over the action.

Finn followed the intimate action, struck by the notion that he'd put the baby inside her. That it was his son, his flesh and blood that blossomed in her belly. 'Baby awake?' he said, feeling awkward again.

Evie looked up, a grimace on her face, which died quickly. Finn was staring at her belly, or rather at the circular motion of her palm, and he seemed so alone and isolated, so untouchable, *so Finn*, way over the other side of the cushion, that it almost tore her breath from her lungs.

'Do you...?' She hesitated, unsure of how

to broach the subject. 'Would you like to feel him moving?' she asked.

Finn mentally recoiled from her quiet suggestion even as his fingers tingled at the possibility. His pulse kicked up a notch. His breath thickened in his throat.

Lay his hands on her? Feel his son moving inside her?

He was used to touching women. Used to touching this woman. But as a prelude to something else. Not like this. Not in a way that bound them beyond just a physical need for release.

He would know his son soon enough. He didn't need to feel his presence to understand his responsibilities.

'Ah, no,' he said, standing, gathering his jacket and his tie and taking a pace back for good measure. 'I'm good.'

Evie tried not to take his rejection personally. They'd taken a big step tonight—she didn't want to scare him away by going all militant mummy on him. 'That's fine,' she said, plastering a smile on her face as she also stood.

They looked at each other, Finn avoiding her belly, Evie fixing on his collar. Finn cursed the sudden uncomfortable silence. The night had gone well—considering.

He cast around for something to say. It seemed only fair, given that he'd been the one to ruin the atmosphere. 'Do you want to have dinner with me tomorrow night?'

Evie blinked. She suddenly felt like a teenager being asked on her first date. 'Ah…yes.'

He nodded. 'I'll pick you up at seven.'

And that set the pattern for the next couple of weeks. Going out or staying in, keeping things light, getting used to just being together without arguing or tearing each other's clothes off. One night Evie pushed a little and asked Finn about his life as a trauma surgeon in the army, and for the longest moment as he hesitated she thought he was going to shut her down, but he didn't and she found herself asking a bit more about it each night. About the places he'd been and the people he'd met.

He was more close-lipped about the specifics, about the horrors he must have seen, but each time he gave away a little more and a little more, even mentioning Isaac's name a couple of times before he realised and then stopped awkwardly and changed the subject.

But for every backward step Evie felt as if they were inching forward and they had plenty of time. She was determined not to push him too far too fast.

* * *

Evie was almost twenty-eight weeks when Finn called one night to say he'd been delayed at the hospital and would miss their restaurant booking. 'How does a spot of telly and a takeaway sound?'

Like an old married couple, she almost said, but, already exhausted from her own full-on shift, she readily agreed.

'I could be a while yet,' he warned.

'Whenever you get here will be fine,' she assured him. She took great delight in kicking off her pregnancy jeans, which she hated, and her bra, which felt like a straitjacket around breasts that seemed to get bigger by the day, and getting into her sloppy pyjamas. The shirt had a tendency to fall off her shoulder and the legs were loose and light. One day soon it wasn't going to meet in the middle but for the moment the ensemble was holding its own.

That was one of the advantages of their unconventional relationship. There was no need to dress to impress. The man had already seen everything she had. She could sloth around in her daggy pyjamas with no bra and no real shape and he was prepared to marry her anyway.

Besides, she didn't think he found her pregnant body much of a turn-on. He'd studiously avoided looking, touching or getting too near her belly. He didn't refer to it, he never remarked about how big she was getting or comment when she rubbed it.

She knew that was partly to do with his issues but she had to face facts—she'd put on some weight, her breasts had doubled in size and her belly had well and truly popped out.

Hardly a sex kitten.

So there seemed very little point making an effort and there was something very comforting about a man who was a sure thing so she threw herself down in front of the telly, her feet up on the coffee table, and waited.

It was nine o'clock when Finn finally knocked and Evie was almost asleep on the couch, but her belly rumbled as she admitted him and she realised she was ravenous. For food and for him. There was something very sexy about the total disregard with which Finn wore a suit. The way he never bothered to do up the jacket so it flapped open all the time or how he couldn't care less about doing up the collar buttons on his shirt and how his tie was always just a little skew. The whole look said, I'd much rather be in scrubs.

Which pretty much summed him up.

He'd brought beer and pizza and they ate it out of the box while he told her about the emergency thoracotomy he'd had to perform on an MVA that had come in after her shift had ended and they watched TV re-runs.

Finn shook his head as Evie laughed at some ridiculous antic. 'I can't believe we're watching this.'

'Hey, I love this show,' Evie protested. 'The nanny used to let us watch it if Lexi and I had done our homework.'

'What about Bella? Didn't she watch it?'

'Of course, but none of them made Bella do anything because of her CF.'

'Poor Bella,' he mused. 'How did she feel about that?'

Evie opened her mouth to give him a flippant reply but it suddenly struck her that Finn was asking *her* about *her* life, seemed interested in *her* life. After two weeks of gently pushing his boundaries back with a feather, he was actually taking an interest in her past.

It was beyond thrilling. She smiled at him. 'She played on it for all she was worth.'

An hour later, with Evie having fallen asleep on his shoulder and snuggled into his side, Finn decided it was time to leave. His arm was numb, which was the stuff his nightmares were made of, and frankly with a large expanse of her cleavage exposed to his view she was just too tempting.

He'd tried not to notice how her body had burgeoned over the last weeks. Tried to concentrate on her, on sticking to his side of the bargain, but her athletic body was developing some fascinating curves, which he'd need to be blind not to notice, given how much time they were spending together.

It was taking all his self-control not to reach for her. To remember she was pregnant. As her bump was getting bigger, it shouldn't have been that difficult but here, now, with her all warm and cosy and smelling fresh and soapy with her hair all loose and her shirt half falling off, exposing the creamy rise of most of one breast and the light from the TV flickering over her skin, it was very difficult.

Finn liked sex. And he was good at it. Even when he'd been practically crippled with pain and numbness in his arm, he'd been good at it.

He and Evie were especially good at it. He reached a plane with her that he'd never reached with anyone else. There'd always been something more than physical. Kind of like what they'd been sharing these last few weeks.

But she was pregnant and they were trying to build a relationship beyond what they already had so making a move on her right now, when things were going so well, was just plain stupid.

He tried to slowly ease away from her but she shifted and murmured and seemed to cling to him even more firmly, pushing her soft breasts into his side.

He prayed for patience, or deliverance.

Whichever came first.

'Evie,' he whispered, and shook her gently, trying really hard not to watch everything jiggling nicely. 'Evie.'

She stirred a little and murmured sleepily. 'Hmm?'

'I'm going to go,' he whispered, trying to ease away again.

Evie dragged herself back from the dark abyss of sleep towards the lure of Finn's whisper. Her eyes fluttered open and her gaze slowly fixed on his face as awareness filtered in. She'd crashed on his shoulder and was smooshed up against him like some crazy stalker.

She removed her hand from his biceps and sat back a little, snuggling her head against the couch instead of his shoulder. She gave him a sleepy, apologetic smile. 'Sorry,' she murmured. 'I'm perpetually tired these days.'

Finn felt the low note of her voice hum along his veins like a tuning fork. 'It's fine,' he said, also keeping his voice low and his gaze firmly trained on her face and not the view straight down her loose top.

'Thanks for the pizza.' She rubbed her belly. 'It was delicious.' The action pulled her shirt down a little more and Evie was surprised to see Finn's eyes widen slightly.

Finn looked. He couldn't help himself. Her breasts were so lush and so...right there. He grimaced as he looked back at her. 'I should... definitely go,' he murmured.

Evie felt her insides dissolve to mush at the look of naked lust she saw heating his gaze to a blue flame. Her hormones, suddenly not sleepy, roared to life. 'You don't have to go,' she said.

Finn sucked in a breath at the shimmer in her soft hazel eyes. 'Evie...'

Evie leaned forward, her breasts tight, her internal muscles quivering in anticipation. 'Stay,' she murmured, and pressed her mouth lightly to his. The beer on his breath was sweet and heady.

Finn, everything north of his groin burning up, groaned the second her lips touched his, ploughing his hands into her hair and deepening the kiss. He pulled back, pressing his forehead against hers as he sucked in air. He felt his control unravelling, as the urge to push her back against the lounge and ravage her pounded through his system. 'I want this too much,' he said on a husky whisper.

'Good,' she breathed, picking up his hand, placing it on her breast and muttering, 'So do I,' as she sought his mouth again.

Finn held her back. 'Wait,' he muttered. 'Not here.' Too many times they'd had rushed sex, hastily parted clothes and a dash to the finish line. Not tonight. Not in her state. He stood and held out his hand. 'Your bedroom.'

Evie would have been perfectly happy with the lounge or the wall or the floor but she was touched by his consideration. But once they hit the bedroom he swept her up and she felt his control shatter on a guttural groan as he kissed her deep and hard.

And then they were pulling at each other's clothes. Shirts and buttons and pants and zippers seemed to melt away as their hands sought bare flesh. And then they were standing before each other naked, his erection jutting between them. His hands brushed against her belly and he pulled away from her, looking down at it, looking down at where his baby was growing. He reached for it again, slid his hands over its rounded contours then slowly up over her breasts, fuller than he remembered, the nipples bigger.

He looked back at her face. 'You're beautiful,' he whispered.

Evie felt beautiful when he looked at her like that. When he touched her so reverently. 'So are you,' she murmured, pressing a kiss to both flat broad pecs.

She trailed her fingers where her mouth had been, trekking up to his shoulders, tracing the scars on his right shoulder before moving down to his biceps. Then slowly shifting, moving around his body until she was standing behind him, her fingers trailing over his back, finding the shrapnel scars she'd only ever felt before, each one breaking her heart a little more.

'Did you get these the day Isaac died?' she asked, dropping a kiss on each one, rubbing her cheek against the puckered skin of his back.

Finn shut his eyes as her kisses soothed and healed. It reminded him of the time she'd tried to offer him solace after he'd lost a patient on the table and for a moment in the operating theatre's change room they'd stood like this, fully dressed, her cheek to his back, him drawing comfort from her simple gesture.

'Evie…'

'I hate it that you were hurt,' she whispered, her lips brushing his skin. 'That you had to go through all that. That your brother was taken from you.'

He opened his mouth to tell her it was a long time ago but it felt as raw right now as it had back then. 'There wasn't anything I could do,' he murmured.

Evie squeezed the tears from her eyes. She'd expected him to say nothing, to clam up. The anguish in his voice was unbearable. She kissed his back. 'I know,' she murmured. 'I know.'

And then she circled back to his front and kissed him with every ounce of passion and compassion she'd ever owned. And then they were on the bed, stroking each other, caressing, kissing and teasing as if they were getting acquainted all over again.

And when they could take it no more Finn looked down at Evie, stroked her belly and said, 'I don't want to hurt you…'

And she hushed him, rolling up on top of him and Finn had never seen anything more beautiful than Evie pregnant with his child, her hair loose, her full breasts bouncing, her belly proud as they moved in a rhythm that was slow and languorous and built to a crescendo that was so sweet Finn knew the sight of Evie flying on the crest of her orgasm would be forever burned into his retinas.

She collapsed on top of him, spent, and he didn't know how long they lay there but at some stage she shifted and he pulled her close, fitting her back against his chest, curling around her, his hand on her belly, kissing her neck, all to the hum of a phenomenal post-coital buzz.

And then he felt the baby move.

And the buzz evaporated.

He waited for something. A bolt of lightning or a beam of light, a trill of excitement—but he got nothing. Life, his own DNA, moved and shifted and grew right under his hand and he felt…nothing.

Panic rose in him. Shouldn't he feel something?

Other than protective? And an overwhelming urge to provide?

Shouldn't he feel love?

Evie, oftentimes oblivious to the baby's movements due to their frequency and this time due to a heavy sexual fog, only became aware of them as she felt Finn tensing around her. She felt him about to withdraw and clamped his hand against her.

'It's okay,' she whispered. 'It's just the baby moving.'

But it wasn't okay and Finn pulled his hand away, eased back from her, rolled up, sat on the side of the bed, cradling his head in his hands.

Evie turned to look at his back, the scars affecting her as deeply as they had just moments ago. She scooted over to where he sat. Her fingers automatically soothed the raised marks and he flinched but didn't pull away, and she kissed each one again as she had earlier. 'What is it Finn? What are you worried about?'

Finn shut his eyes. He wanted to push her away but her gentleness was his undoing. 'Something died in me the day I got these scars, Evie. The day Isaac died. I don't think I'm capable of love.'

He heard her start to protest and forced himself to open his eyes, forced his legs to work as he broke away to stand and look down at her, gloriously naked, her belly full of his baby.

'I'm worried I'm not going to love him.'

Evie smiled at him gently. 'Of course you will. That's what parents do.'

Finn shook his head and the sadness in his eyes cut her even deeper than his scars had. 'Not all of them, Evie.'

CHAPTER EIGHT

EVIE DRAGGED HERSELF through the next few days. She hadn't seen Finn since he'd picked up his clothes and left the other night and there was a small part of her that was beginning to despair that she might never be able to reach him.

But after three punishing day shifts in a row she was too exhausted to care when she crawled into bed at eight-thirty and turned off the bedside lamp. Her feet ached, her back ached and she wanted to shut her eyes and sleep for a week.

She'd worry about Finn tomorrow.

Except that wasn't to be.

Evie woke from a deep, dark sleep with a start several hours later, a feeling of dread pushing against her chest. Her heart was racing. Something was wrong but for a moment she couldn't figure out what.

As she lay in the dark, the luminous figures on the clock telling her it was two-thirteen a.m., she slowly became aware of a feeling of wetness. She reached down, her hand meeting a warm, wet puddle. Had she wet herself?

Before she could apply any logical thought process, a spasm that caused her to cry out and clutch at her belly, pulsed through her deep and low.

Was she bleeding?

The pain eased and panic drove her into a sitting position as she kicked off the sheet and reached for the light, snapping it on. The bed was saturated, clear liquid soaking into the sheets and mattress, her wet pyjama pants clinging to her legs.

Her pulse hammered madly at her temples as she tried to think.

Clear. Not blood. And a lot of it.

Not urine. Too much. She hadn't the bladder capacity for more than a thimbleful for what seemed for ever.

Another pain ripped through her and she gasped as it tore her breath away and she suddenly realised it was amniotic fluid in the bed.

Her membranes had ruptured.

And she was in labour.

The spasm held her in its grip for what

seemed an age and Evie failed miserably at doing all the things she knew you were supposed to do during a contraction—stay calm, breathe deeply—by intermittently crying and then holding her breath to try and stop herself from crying.

She collapsed on her side, reaching for the phone on the bedside table as soon as she was able, quickly stabbing Finn's number into the touchpad. It rang in her ear and she hoped like crazy that he had the same special powers that every other doctor who spent half of their lives on call possessed—the ability to wake to a ringing phone in a nanosecond.

He picked up on the third ring but she didn't give him a chance to utter a greeting. 'Finn!' she sobbed. 'It's Evie. My membranes have ruptured. I'm contracting.' As if to prove her point the next contraction came and she almost choked as she doubled up, trying to talk and gasp and groan all at the same time. 'The baby…is coming…now!'

'I'll be there in one minute.'

But she didn't hear him as the phone slipped from her fingers and she curled in a ball, rocking and crying as the uterine spasm grabbed hold and squeezed so tight Evie felt like she was going to split open.

It was too early. The baby would be too small. She couldn't do this. She wasn't ready. The baby wasn't ready.

She heard Finn belting on her door a minute later and she cried out to him but the contractions were coming one on top of the other, paralysing her. She just couldn't get up and open it. She was conscious of a loud crash and Finn calling out her name, his voice getting closer and closer, and she cried out to him again and suddenly he was stalking into her bedroom.

Finn was shocked at the sight that confronted him. Evie—strong, competent, assured Evie—curled up in a ball on the bed, her pyjama pants soaking, her face and eyes red from crying, a look of sheer panic on her face.

He threw himself down beside her. 'Evie!'

'Finn,' Evie sobbed clutching at his shirt-sleeve, her hand shaking. 'Help me,' she begged. 'It's too early. Don't let our baby die.'

The words chilled him, so similar to the words Isaac had used as he'd reached out a bloodied hand to Finn.

Finn! Finn! Help me. Don't let me die.

Words that had haunted him for a decade. The promise that he'd given haunting him for just as long. One he hadn't been able to keep in the middle of hell, injured as he'd been and with precious medical help too far away.

But he could make a promise right here and now that he could keep. Last time he'd been powerless to help.

But not this time.

'I won't,' he promised. 'I won't.' He was damned if he was going to let down another person he cared about.

He stood and dragged the light summer blanket that had fallen off the end of Evie's bed away from the mattress and wrapped it around her then scooped her up as she moaned in pain and sobbed her heart out.

There was no point in ringing an ambulance—he could be there in three minutes at this hour of night.

He strode out the door he'd damaged trying to get in and pulled it shut behind him—he'd get the lock fixed later. The lift arrived within seconds and a minute later she was ensconced in his car and he was driving out of the garage. He dialled the emergency department and got the triage nurse.

'This is Finn Kennedy. I'm three minutes out with Evie Lockheart, who has gone into premature labour at twenty-eight weeks. I need the neonatal resus team there stat.'

He hung up and dialled another number, zoning Evie's anguish out, doing what he had to do, drumming his fingers on the steering-wheel as he sped through a deserted red light.

The phone was picked up. 'Marco? It's Finn Kennedy. Evie's gone into labour. I'm two minutes out from the hospital. The baby is coming now.'

Whether it was that particular note of urgency one doctor recognised in another or the background noise of Evie's distress, Finn wasn't sure, but Marco's 'I'll be there in ten' was all he needed to hear before he hung up.

He glanced at Evie and reached for her hand. 'Everything's ready. The neonatal team will be there and Marco's on his way. We're a minute out.' He squeezed her hand. 'Hold on, okay?'

Evie squeezed back as contractions battered her body. She knew she was a snivelling mess, she knew she shouldn't be, that she should be calm and rational and confident in modern medicine and the stats on premmie births, but fear pounded through every cell, rendering her incapable of reason.

Right now she was a mother. And she was terrified.

Finn screeched into the ambulance bay fifty-five seconds later. Mia and Luca were there with two nurses and a gurney, and they had a hysterical Evie inside in a cubicle within a minute. The neonatal team was already there, a high-tech cot with its warming lamps on ready to accept the baby, and Finn suddenly felt superfluous as the team went into action around him.

He felt lost. Outside his body, looking down. Usually in an emergency situation in a hospital setting *he* was the one in control. But not now. Right now he could do nothing but just stand around helplessly and watch.

Just like with Isaac.

'Finn!'

Evie's wretched wail as she looked around for him brought him back to the present, to the trilling of alarms, to the hive of activity.

'I'm here,' he said, stepping closer, claiming a position near her head, reaching for her searching hand. They weren't in the dirt in the middle of a battle zone and she wasn't dying. They were at Sydney Harbour Hospital with as good a medical team around them as anywhere in the world and she wasn't dying. 'I'm right here.'

The curtain snapped back and Marco entered, and Finn knew everything was going to be fine. 'Well, Evie,' Marco said in that accented way of his, 'this is unexpected but don't worry, you are in very good hands.'

Evie was grateful Marco was there but the feeling was swept away by a sudden over-whelming urge to push. She half sat forward, dislodging two monitoring electrodes and causing a cacophony of alarms to go off. 'I need to push,' she said, the noise escalating her panic to full-scale terror.

Marco nodded. 'Don't push, Evie,' he said calmly as he snapped on a pair of gloves. 'Pant. Let me just check you.'

Evie gritted her teeth. 'I…can't…' she groaned as her abdomen contracted of its own accord.

Finn leaned in close to her ear, kissed her temple and said, 'Yes, you can, Evie. Yes you can. Here, do it with me,' he said, as he panted.

Evie squeezed his hand harder, fighting against the dictates of her body, trying hard to pant and be productive and not let the panic win.

'Okay, the baby is crowning,' Marco said.

'No,' Evie pleaded. 'No, no, no.' She turned to Finn, clutching their joined hands to her chest. 'It's too soon, he's too small.'

'And he's in the best place,' Finn said, hop-ing it was the right thing to say, the thing she needed to hear. He wished he could take the fear and anguish from her eyes. That he could take her physical pain and bear it for her. 'And we're all going to fight for him.'

'Okay Evie, let's meet your son,' Marco said.

Evie cried and shook her head, still trying to stop it, to hold inside her the precious baby who needed more time, but the urge coming over her again couldn't be denied and although she didn't assist, she couldn't fight it either, and because the baby was so small he slipped out into Marco's waiting hands in one smooth movement.

'Got him!' Marco exclaimed, as he quickly clamped and cut the cord and passed the still newborn into the warmed sterile dressing towel held by the neonatologist.

'He's a good size,' Marco said, looking up at Evie.

Finn and Evie only vaguely heard him as they both held their breath, straining to hear a little cry through the rush and hurry around them.

'He's not crying,' Evie murmured.

Finn kissed her forehead as the suction was turned on. 'Give it a sec.'

But there was still no gurgling first baby cry. No annoyed, indignant wail at having a plastic tube shoved up its nose. They could hear terms like *bradycardic* and *low sats* and *starting compressions* and *get an IV* and *need to tube him* and Evie turned her face into Finn's shoulder and cried, quietly this time, as a scenario she'd been part of on many occasions played out.

Only this time it wasn't some anonymous person off the street—it was happening to her.

'He's going to be fine,' Finn said, his head close to hers. 'He's going to be fine.'

If he said it enough times, it might just be true.

Then he heard *I'm in* and he looked up as the tone of the sats monitor changed. *Sats improving. Heart rate picking up.*

He kissed Evie on the head. 'They've tubed him,' he whispered. 'He's improving.'

Evie looked up, the normal sound of the sats monitor like music to her ears. She turned her head towards the flurry of activity around the cot. 'How's he doing?' he asked.

The neonatologist turned around. 'He was a little flat. He needed some help with his breathing—not unusual at twenty-eight weeks. Hopefully we can get him straight on to CPAP. We'll put in an umbi line and given him some steroids down the ETT. We'll take him up to the unit now, it's the best place for him.'

Evie nodded vigorously. 'Of course, go, take him,' she urged. She wanted him in the best place, with the best people looking after him, but she couldn't deny how bereft she felt. She'd given birth to him but she hadn't even touched her little boy yet or seen his face.

Her arms ached to hold him. To be near him right now.

She turned to Finn. 'Go with them,' she said.

Finn frowned. 'What? No Evie, he's in good hands, I'll stay with you until you're settled upstairs and then I'll go and check on him.'

Evie, feeling strong now, dashed at the moisture clinging to her cheeks. 'I don't want him up there by himself, Finn.'

'He's going to be surrounded by people,' Finn said gently.

'No.' She shook her head vehemently. 'Not people who love him. That is our son up there and I want him to know that every second of every day we're right beside him. Go, please, please go. If you don't, Finn, I swear to God I will, placenta delivered or not.'

Finn caught the eye of Marco, who indicated with a quick flick of his head to hop to it. But he was torn. He wanted to be with his son, but he didn't want to abandon Evie either.

Evie grabbed his sleeve. 'I'm going to be fine,' she said. 'I'm sorry, I know I've been a mess tonight but I'm fine now. And I need you to do this. Promise me you'll stay with him until I can get there.'

Finn blinked at the zealous glow in Evie's eyes that turned them from soft hazel to a supernatural hue. He nodded, knowing it was another promise he could keep. 'I promise,' he murmured. 'But don't be long.'

Evie gave a half-laugh. 'I'll try. Now go!' she urged as the cot and the team headed out of the cubicle.

Finn stopped by Marco, who was pulling gently on the umbilical cord to deliver the placenta. 'I have my mobile. Call me as soon as you're done here.'

Marco nodded. *'Assolutamente.'*

Five hours later Ava strode into the isolation room they'd put little baby Lockheart in because there were some perks to being on staff and because they were quiet enough at the moment to allow it. Not that it was exactly isolated—large windows on three sides kept it fully visible to the entire unit.

She smiled at the nurse making notes on a computer console before spying Finn sitting in a chair beside the open cot, valiantly trying to keep his eyes open, his head bobbing up and down as he intermittently lost the battle before regaining control.

'Finn,' she said bending down to push her face closer to him when he didn't seem to register her presence.

He looked as if he'd been pulled through a hedge backwards. His jeans had a stain down the front and his shirt looked like it had been crumpled in a ball in the corner for a week. His stubbly look was bordering on haggard. His feet were bare.

Finn shook his head as his name was called again and the figure in front of him came into focus. 'Ava.'

She pushed a takeaway coffee towards him. 'You specialise in looking like hell, don't you?'

He gave a half-smile, accepting her offering gratefully. 'Only for you.'

Ava looked at the cot, seeing more tubes than baby. 'Big night, I hear.'

Finn nodded. He stood and looked down at

his son, who had rapidly improved in just a few hours and was now only on CPAP via the ventilator to lightly support his own breathing rather than the machine doing the breathing for him.

'This is just the half of it. Evie needed a manual removal of her placenta then part of it was left behind so she had to have a D and C as well. She only got back to her room at six.' He still felt sick thinking about the fist that had squeezed a handful of his gut when Marco had come to tell him the news personally.

Ava nodded. 'I know. I've just come from there.'

Finn looked up, eager for firsthand news of her. 'You have? How's she going?'

'She's sleeping. Bella's with her.'

Finn nodded. He had called Bella a couple of hours ago because he didn't want Evie to be alone. Lexi had been his first instinct but she was also dealing with a newborn and he figured she needed the sleep more. Bella had popped in briefly to see the baby, taken a picture, then gone to her sister.

'Evie made me promise not to leave him until she got here.'

Ava smiled. 'Of course she did. She's a mum now. And what about you? How are you feeling now he's here and it's all a little more real?'

Finn shook his head. 'More like surreal.' He looked down at his tiny son, just over one kilo, everything in miniature but all still in perfect working order. His chest rose and fell robustly despite his little bird-like ribcage and his pulse oximeter bleeped away steadily in the background, picking up the strong, sure beating of his heart.

'I'm scared. Worried. Petrified.'

'But he's doing well, yes?'

Finn nodded. 'But I keep thinking about all the possibilities. Immature lungs. Intracranial haemorrhages. Infection. Jaundice. Cardiac complications. I can't breathe when I think of all the things that can go wrong.'

'Well, that's one of the hazards of knowing just a little too much, I guess. But this little tyke is probably stronger than you think. He's a tough guy, just like his daddy.'

Finn felt his heart contract and then expand so much it felt like it was filling his chest, the cold bands that had clamped around it the day Isaac had died shattering into a thousand pieces. He gazed at his son. 'I love him more than I thought it possible to love anything.'

Ava smiled. 'Of course, you're a dad now.'

* * *

Three hours later Finn was watching his son take his first breaths off the ventilator. He'd done so well the team had extubated him and popped on some high-flow humidified nasal prongs. He'd fussed at first, his little hoarse squawk pinging Finn's protective strings, but with a couple of sleepy blinks he'd settled and was, once again, getting on with the business of breathing unassisted.

Finn was watching his son through the open cot's glass side panel when he heard some squeaking behind him and turned around to find Bella pushing her sister into the room in a wheelchair.

'Evie?' Finn stood, shocked by her pallor, covering the two steps separating them quickly, sinking to his knees in front of the wheelchair. She had dark rings under her eyes and her lips were dry. 'Are you okay? I don't think you should be out of bed.'

'She shouldn't be,' Bella agreed. 'But she threatened to pull her drip out and make a run for it if I didn't bring her.'

'I'm fine,' Evie dismissed. Nothing else mattered to her right now more than seeing her baby. The little boy who'd been impatient to make his entry into the world.

He'd been the first thing on her mind when she'd woken from her anaesthetic and after letting weariness, exhaustion and well-intentioned people fob her off for the last few hours, she'd made her stand.

'Push me closer, Bells,' Evie demanded, bouncing in her seat a little, trying to get a better view. If she'd thought she could walk and not faint, she'd have been by his side already.

Finn stood. 'Here. Let me.'

Bella stepped back. 'I'll give you two some privacy,' she said. 'Ring me, Finn, when Evie's ready to go back and I can take her, or I can sit with the baby for a while if you like so you can stretch your legs.'

Finn nodded his thanks and pushed Evie over to the cot side. 'Here he is,' he murmured. 'Master Impatient.'

Evie felt tears well in her eyes, overwhelmed by the fragile little human being they'd created dwarfed by the medical technology around him. He was wearing the tiniest disposable nappy Evie had ever seen and a little blue beanie. He looked like a doll and the mother in her wanted to scoop him up, clutch him to her breast, slay anyone who dared come near him, but the doctor knew he was better off right where he was for now.

She flattened her palm against the glass, too low in the chair to be able to reach in and too sore and weak to be able to stand but feeling the strength of their connection anyway. Their unbreakable bond.

'Hello, baby, I'm your mummy,' she whispered.

And she listened as Finn pulled up a chair beside her and recounted what had happened since they'd left her in the department. About how their son had improved in leaps and bounds and how incredibly stable his blood gases and body temp and sugar levels had been.

'He's done everything right, Evie.' Finn placed a hand on her knee. 'He's a real little fighter.'

Evie nodded, tears blurring her vision. 'Of course,' she said, placing a hand over his and giving him a squeeze. She looked at him. 'He's just like his daddy.'

Finn's heart almost broke at the shimmer of tears in her eyes. He never wanted her to hurt again. He'd watch her go through hell last night and then she'd gone through even more without him, and he didn't want to ever be away from her again. He wanted to wrap them both up and love them for ever.

Finn turned his hand over and intertwined their fingers. 'According to your father, he has the Lockheart brow.'

Evie laughed. 'My father's been?'

Finn nodded. 'He and your mother called in briefly earlier. She agreed.'

'My mother?' They'd been making some inroads to their relationship in the last months since Bella had received her new lungs but Evie knew there was still a long way to go.

'Well, they're both wrong,' she said, gazing at her son's tiny face. Even all wizened, she could see the mark of Kennedy genes everywhere. 'He has *your* brow. *And* your chin. *And* your nose. I don't know about those fabulous cheekbones, though…'

Finn stared at them as he'd been doing for the last eight hours, trying not to remember why they were so familiar. 'They're Isaac's,' he whispered, finally admitting it. 'According to Lydia, Isaac had cheekbones that belonged in Hollywood.'

Evie glanced at him. His voice was tinged with sadness and humour and regret. 'I'm sorry he never got to see his nephew,' she whispered, holding tight to his hand.

Finn nodded. 'So am I. He'd have been a great uncle.'

And for the first time in a long time he remembered the happy times he and Isaac had shared instead of how it had all ended, and he could smile. How Isaac had always managed to find a baby to cuddle or a toddler to give a piggy-back ride to, wherever they'd ended up.

The baby squirmed, making a mewling noise like a tiny kitten and waving his little fists, no bigger than gumballs, in the air, dislodging a chest electrode and tripping an alarm. Evie's gaze flew to the cot, her pulse spiking as a moment of fear gripped her, suddenly understanding how nerve-racking it must be for her patients to be in an unfamiliar environment with strange machines that made alarming noises.

'It's okay,' the nurse said, unconcerned, as she pushed the alarm silence button. 'Just lost a dot.'

She located the AWOL chest lead and replaced it back just below a collarbone that looked to Evie as spindly as a pipe cleaner. 'There we go, little darling,' the nurse crooned. 'All fixed.' She smiled at Finn and Evie. 'Is there a name yet? Because we can call him little darling for ever but he might get teased when he goes to school,' she joked.

Evie looked at Finn and then back at the nurse. 'We hadn't got that far,' she said helplessly, already feeling like she'd failed her

AMY ANDREWS
221

tiny little son twice. Once for not being able
to keep him inside where he'd desperately
needed to stay for a good while longer and
now not having a name to give to him.

'Well, there's no rush,' she murmured. 'But
a wee little guy like this needs a warrior's
name, I reckon.'

Evie couldn't agree more and as the nurse
fussed over the lines in the cot she knew with
sudden clarity what to call him. 'Isaac,' she
said to the nurse. 'His name's Isaac.'

The nurse smiled. 'Isaac,' she repeated.
'Ooh, that's good. Strong. Noble.' She looked
down at the tiny baby in her care and said,
'Welcome to the world, Isaac.'

Evie smiled through another spurt of tears
as the nurse bustled away. She turned to face
Finn. 'Is that okay with you?'

Finn's chest was so tight he thought it
might just implode from the pressure. He was
shocked to feel moisture stinging his eyes
and a lump in his throat that barely allowed
for the passage of air. He forced himself to
look at her instead of turning away or blinking the tears back, like he'd done for so many
years. He couldn't even remember the last
time he'd allowed himself to cry. Not even
as the life had ebbed from his brother's eyes
had he broken down.

He'd just shut down. Gone numb.

And it had taken this woman and this tiny scrap of humanity to bring him back.

'I think that would be quite wonderful,' he whispered, his voice thick with emotion.

'But could you hear it every day, Finn?' she probed, her voice gentle. 'Would it make you sad every day?'

Finn shook his head. 'No. I've spent a decade of my life trying to forget what happened and all I've managed to do is erase all the good things as well. I think it's time I remembered them also.'

Evie nodded, squeezing her hand. It sounded like a damn fine plan to her. 'Do you think Lydia will mind?'

Finn smiled. 'I think she'd be delighted.'

'Good,' Evie murmured. 'Good. Isaac it is.'

They smiled at each other for a long moment then turned to gaze lovingly at their son. Finn slid a hand onto Evie's shoulder. 'I've been such an idiot,' he said as he watched Isaac's little puffy breaths kick his rib cage up and down.

'You were grieving,' Evie dismissed, also watching her son, trying to absorb every tiny detail about him.

'I don't mean that. I mean about what I said the other night. After we'd…'

'Oh,' Evie said, glancing at his profile. 'That.'

'All I have to do is look at him and I feel this incredible surge of love rise in me.' Finn didn't take his eyes off Isaac's face. 'And I don't even know where it comes from or that I even had it in me but I do know that it's deep and wide and unfathomable and if I live to be a hundred I'd never get to the bottom of it.'

He looked at Evie then and she was watching him so intently, and he needed her to know, to understand so she could never, ever doubt that he loved Isaac. 'I was so, so worried that I wouldn't, Evie. I was terrified. But it's like…it's just there. It's suddenly just there.'

Evie felt his relief and wonder and even though she'd never really doubted that he would feel this way about his own flesh in blood he'd been so bleak, so convinced the other night when he'd left that she'd felt her first prickle of unease.

She smiled at him. 'I know.'

'It's like a…miracle.' He laughed. 'This love is like a bloody miracle. It's so different from anything I've ever felt before.'

Evie smiled but it felt forced in comparison to his obvious high. She was ecstatic that he knew what she'd always known—that he'd take to fatherhood, revel in it even. But part of her wished a little of that miracle was coming her way.

That he'd look at her and talk about the miracle of the love he felt for her. A very different love from what he was talking about now.

Because while Isaac needed Finn's love, so did she. The kind of love that would fill her soul and warm her days.

A man's love for a woman.

'And you,' Finn said, shaking his head, in awe of what she'd been through. 'You are amazing. Incredible. What your body has done is truly awesome.' He looked at his son, so small but so perfect. 'Isaac and I are so lucky to have you and I'm going to spend the rest of my life taking care of you. Nothing... nothing will be too good for the mother of my child. I love you, Evie,' he said, watching Isaac. 'I couldn't have picked a more perfect mother if I'd tried.'

Evie's breath caught at the words she'd been waiting to hear ever since they'd met at that hospital function five years ago. And they felt so empty.

He was on his daddy high and she was the mother of his child swept up in the raw newness of him coming inside after a long cold winter.

Suddenly she felt overwhelmingly tired.

CHAPTER NINE

AN HOUR LATER, after Evie had expressed for the first time and they'd watch one mil of milk disappear down the gastric tube Finn had insisted that Evie go back to bed. She looked exhausted, the black rings around her eyes had increased, her shoulders had drooped and she was sleep staring at everything with long slow sleepy blinks.

He made a mental note to check her haemoglobin with Marco when he saw him later.

'What about you?' she protested. 'You've been up since two with no sleep.'

'Yes, but I haven't given birth or had an emergency operation. I'll catch some sleep tonight in my office if everything stays stable.' He'd spent many a night on the surprisingly comfortable couch.

It felt wrong to leave Isaac but Bella and Lexi had eagerly volunteered to keep vigil while he pushed Evie back to her room and he had to admit it felt good to be out, stretching his legs.

She was quiet on the trip and his concern for her condition ramped up to another level. 'Are you okay?' he asked as he pulled the wheelchair up beside her bed, crouching down in front of her. 'Have you got pain? Do you feel unwell?' He placed his palm on her forehead, checking for a temperature.

Evie shut her eyes, allowing herself to lean into his hand for a few seconds. 'I'm fine,' she said, avoiding his gaze as she opened her eyes again. 'Just tired.'

He frowned as she seemed to evade eye contact. It seemed more than that. 'You need to be rested and well for your milk production.'

Evie blinked. As a doctor, she understood what he was saying was correct. She'd told many a patient exactly that and she had the pamphlet in her hand to back it up. But it wasn't what she wanted to hear him say. She wanted him to hug her, rub her back and tell her she was beautiful.

Which, of course, he wouldn't, first because he was Finn and, second, she really wasn't beautiful, more classically interesting, and last she doubted she'd ever looked worse. Although she guessed it didn't really matter what you looked like when you'd stopped being a woman and become the milk supply line for a premmie baby.

'I see you're going to be the milk police,' she said, her voice brittle.

Finn chose his words carefully to her irritable response. There *was* something bugging her. 'Colostrum is vital for Isaac's immune system.'

Evie took a steadying breath as despair and animosity battled it out inside her. This was typical Finn in tunnel-vision medical mode. All about the facts.

'Yes, I know,' she said, scooting him aside so she could crawl onto her freshly made bed. She almost groaned out loud as the crisp white sheets melted against her skin like snowflakes and all her cells sighed in unison.

Finn stood up and watched as Evie's eyes fluttered shut. He had the distinct feeling she was trying to block him out. 'Evie…?'

He hesitated, not really knowing how to voice his concerns to a woman who was probably experiencing a hormone surge not unlike Chernobyl's meltdown. Even if he did love her.

'You seem…down…and you know PND can start very early post-partum and it's particularly high in mothers with premmies.'

Evie sighed. *There he went with the facts again.* 'Finn,' she said sharply, opening her eyes and piercing him with her cranky hazel gaze. 'I've just given birth to a twenty-eight-weeker who's in the NICU and I'm two floors away. I feel like an utter failure and my arms *literally* ache to hold him. Yes, I'm *down*. No, I *do not* have postnatal depression.'

Finn sat on the side of the bed. 'Oh, Evie...' He reached for her hand.

Evie really did not want to be pitied so she evaded his reach. 'Look, just go, will you, Finn? Go back to Isaac. I'm tired and not thinking straight. I'm sure I'll feel a lot better after a sleep.'

Finn opened his mouth to say something but Marco entered the room, greeting them in his usual jovial way. 'How are you feeling, Evie?'

'Tired,' Finn murmured.

Evie glared at him. 'A little tired, otherwise fine.'

'What's her haemoglobin, Marco?' Finn asked.

'Ten point nine,' Marco said, not having to consult the chart in his hands. 'She lost very little blood,' he assured Finn, before turning to Evie and asking a couple more questions. 'I think we take down that drip now and discharge you tomorrow morning if everything goes well overnight.'

Evie nodded, feeling ridiculously teary again at the thought of going home without Isaac. 'I won't be going far,' she said.

'Which makes me even more comfortable with discharging you.' Marco smiled.

They chatted for a while longer, talking about Isaac, and Marco smiling over his own little one's antics before he noticed Evie yawn. 'I better get on,' he said. 'I'll see you in the morning.'

Finn stood and shook his hand. 'Thanks, Marco. You were brilliant last night.'

'Yes,' Evie agreed. 'You were fabulous. I'll never forget how you came in when you weren't on call.'

Marco winked at her. 'Anything for Evie Lockheart.'

Finn rolled his eyes. 'I bet you say that to all your mothers.'

Evie shut her eyes as Marco chuckled and Finn once again relegated her to a role instead of a person. Would he ever see her as a woman again? Love her as a woman? Or would he always just love her because she was the mother of his child?

'But thanks,' Finn continued. 'Evie's right. I owe you.'

Marco chuckled. 'I hope that is something I never have to collect on. My cholesterol is good and there is no cardiac history in my family.'

'Well, how about I buy you a beer at Pete's as soon as Isaac is home instead?'

Marco nodded. 'It's a deal. Although let's make it a red wine instead—just to be sure.'

Marco left and Evie faked a yawn. She had the sudden urge to bury her head under the covers and not come out. Maybe Finn was right. Maybe she was going through those baby blues a little early.

'I'll go too,' he said, satisfied to see her already look a little less exhausted around her eyes, even if she did seem to still be avoiding eye contact. He sat on the side of the bed again. 'Ring me after you've had a sleep and I can come back and get you.'

Evie nodded, a lump in her throat at the tenderness in his voice. Then he leaned forward and pressed a chaste kiss on her forehead. He stood and said, 'I love you, Evie,' before walking out the door.

Evie let the tears come then. She wasn't sure what had been more heartbreaking, his throwaway line about loving her or the kiss currently air-drying on her forehead. His declaration of love—his second—was about as heartfelt as that kiss. Something he might bestow on an aged great-aunt with whiskers growing out of her chin.

Asexual. Perfunctionary. Expected.

Was that what she had to look forward to now she was a *mother*? Some idealised figure who was a nurturer. And nothing else?

Finn was going to put her on some bloody pedestal and turn her into something holy and untouchable.

After a full night's sleep Evie was almost feeling human again at barely five a.m. as she crept down to the NICU by herself to visit with her little man and do some more expressing. Finn was there, still maintaining his vigil beside Isaac's incubator, and for a moment she just stood in the doorway, watching him watch their son.

Her heart squeezed painfully in her chest at the sight. She could feel Finn's love for Isaac rolling off him in waves, encompassing the cot and the tiny little scrap of humanity inside it as if he was the most precious child that had ever lived. The area around the cot practically glowed with the force field of Finn's love.

It was exactly what she'd wanted. And yet she was suddenly incredibly jealous.

Which was selfish, hateful and greedy.

And she had to let it go because their son needed her to concentrate on him and his needs and the long haul ahead. Not on any insecurities over Finn. And this morning at least she was feeling more in charge of herself to do just that.

She shuffled forward in her slippers and slid her hand onto Finn's shoulder. He turned and looked up at her and he looked so weary and sexy she plastered a smile on her face.

'Morning,' she murmured. 'How's our little warrior?'

Finn smiled back, hopping out of his chair for her to sit in. 'He's doing well. They've reduced his oxygen. He's coping.'

'Did you sleep?' she asked.

'No,' the nurse piped up.

'I dozed on and off,' Finn corrected her.

Evie looked up at him standing beside her. He looked like he hadn't slept in a hundred years—his lines had lines. 'You look exhausted,' she said.

'I'm fine.' Finn brushed his tiredness aside. '*You*, on the other hand, look much, much better.'

'I feel a hundred per cent better,' she admitted.

Finn squeezed her shoulder. He'd been worried about her yesterday but she looked like the old Evie and he felt one of his worries lift. 'Good.'

'In fact…' Evie stood, gently reaching out and stroking Isaac's closest arm, the warm fuzz covering it tickling her finger '…I'm going to go and express then I'm going to come back here and stay until Marco's round at eleven for my discharge and then I'm coming straight back. So I want you to go and catch up on some sleep.'

Finn looked at the determined set to Evie's chin and felt that protective part of him that had refused to let him leave Isaac's side relax as it recognised the strength of Evie's protective instinct. 'Okay. I'll go to my office and have a couple of hours.'

Evie shook her head. 'Finn, you need a shower, a decent meal and a proper bed. Go home. Rest properly.'

He shook his head. 'I can't leave you sitting here all day. Not so soon after your discharge. You need the rest more than I do.'

Yeah, yeah. The milk. But she let it go, refusing to dwell on something that was fact anyway.

'It's okay. Bella and Lexi will be in and out fussing around all day, making me go for walks and feeding me well. And seeing as your theatre cases have been reassigned this week, I'll let you take the night shift again.'

Finn laughed. 'Why, thank you.'

He hesitated. The offer was tempting. He'd been in the same clothes for almost thirty-six hours. And they hadn't been clean to begin with. If it hadn't been for Ava persuading Gladys to let her into his apartment, he probably still wouldn't have shoes. He'd used the toothpaste and toothbrush from the care pack he'd been given by one of the NICU nurses.

A shower and his own bed did sound mighty tempting.

He looked down at Isaac and felt torn. What if something went wrong while he was away? He'd been rock-steady stable but Isaac was in NICU for a reason.

'I promise I'll call immediately if anything happens,' Evie murmured, sensing his conflict and knowing it intimately. How much had she fretted during the hours she'd spent away from him?

'Okay,' he said, giving in to the dictates of his utterly drained body. 'Thanks.'

Finn was back at three o'clock. He'd eaten, showered, slept like a log for two hours longer than he'd planned and zipped quickly into town to do something he should have done weeks ago. Then he'd left his car back at Kirribilli Views and walked to the hospital. It was a nice day and it gave him a chance to think things through, to plan. He stopped in at the canteen on his way to the unit and bought two coffees and some snack supplies for later tonight.

'Hi, there,' he said, striding into Evie's room.

She looked up from changing Isaac's nappy. It was the first time she'd touched him properly and even though it was a thick, black, meconium bowel motion, she was vibrating with excitement. Perfectly functioning bowels were another cause for celebration.

'Poo!' she announced to Finn. 'Who'd have ever thought you could be so happy about a dirty nappy!'

Finn caught his breath. Her eyes were sparkling and she looked deliriously happy. He didn't understand why it had taken him so long to figure out he loved her when just thinking about her now made his heart grow bigger in his chest.

He laughed, understanding an excitement that might seem bizarre to others. 'That's our boy,' he said.

Lexi, who was also in the room, shook her head and pronounced them nuts.

Evie finished up and Finn hovered nearby,

talking to his son, whose eyes fluttered open from time to time indignantly as his sleep was disturbed. When she was done he passed her the coffee, gave his to Lexi and they filled him in on the day, including the news that the oxygen had been reduced even further.

'He's a little marvel!' Lexi exclaimed.

Finn couldn't have agreed more and to see Evie with her eyes glittering and her skin glowing was a sight for sore eyes.

'You're just in time,' Evie said. 'I was about to go and express. You can entertain Lexi.'

Finn glanced up. 'Actually, would you mind going solo for a bit, Lex? I wouldn't mind having a chat with your sister.' He looked at Evie. 'If that's okay with you?'

Evie felt her breath catch a little at the intensity in his blue, blue gaze. She'd forgotten with all the madness of the last couple of days and a side whammy of maternal hormones how it could reach right inside her and stroke her.

Was she okay with him watching her express? It should have been an easy answer—it wasn't like he hadn't seen her naked before. They'd made Isaac together, for crying out loud. But she hesitated anyway. It was pretty damn obvious he'd already relegated her to mother status—surely that would only enhance his opinion more?

Lexi noticed her hesitation. 'Why don't you let the poor woman and her leaking breasts be, Finn Kennedy? I won't bite and after she's done I'll stick around so you can take Evie outside and talk without the slurp and suck of a breast pump serenading you.'

Finn looked at Evie. He could tell she was relived at her sister's intervention and he didn't know what that meant exactly. He'd felt on the same page with her during their getting to know each other weeks but due to the rather dramatic interruption of Isaac's early arrival he wasn't sure about anything any more.

He was, however, grateful for a little bit of sanity from Lexi. What had he been thinking? Breast-pump music was not the ambience he was after.

'Of course.' He smiled. 'Good plan.'

Forty-five minutes later Finn and Evie were ensconced in a booth at Pete's. He'd chosen it over the canteen for its relative quietness at this time of the day. Weekday hospital staff didn't tend to arrive until after six o'clock so they had plenty of time to be uninterrupted. Unlike the canteen, where they'd have been swamped with well-wishers, their conversation stifled.

And he could do without their private life being aired on the grapevine—for once.

'So I was thinking,' Finn said as he placed a sparkling water in a wine glass in front of her and a Coke in front of him, 'that you should move into the penthouse with me while we're getting the Lavender Bay house set up.'

Evie, who had chosen that moment to take a sip of her drink, almost choked as she half-inhaled it in shock. She coughed and spluttered for a while, trying to rid the irritation of sparkling water from her trachea.

'Is it that shocking?' Finn joked as he waited for her to settle.

'Yes,' she rasped, clearing her throat and taking another sip of water.

Finn reached across the table and covered Evie's hands with his. 'It makes sense to me. We'll be getting married as soon as Isaac is home and as we both live in the same building anyway, it seems silly to keep two places going.'

Evie looked down at their joined hands as the very practical reasons for her moving in with him sank in. 'Right,' she murmured. She had to admit he made good sense even if it had been thought about in that logical way of Finn's.

But…where was the emotion?

The *I can't live without you one more day.* The *I love you, never leave my side.*

She drew her hands out from under his. 'Finn…I don't think this is something we should be worrying about at the moment. I just want to focus on Isaac. On what he needs.'

Finn felt her withdrawal reach deep inside him. He knew she was right, that Isaac had to come first, but they also had to look after themselves. There was no point being run down from stress and lack of sleep when Isaac finally came home.

Home.

The word resonated inside him and settled easily, warming him from the inside out instead of echoing around all the lonely places as it always had.

He had a home. And a family to share it with.

'You still need a base, Evie. A place to have a quick shower and change your clothes, lay your head for a few hours maybe, collect your mail…that kind of thing.'

She nodded. 'Fleeting visits, yes. But I plan to spend as much time on the unit with Isaac as I can without totally exhausting myself. I can't bear to think of him there all by himself, Finn.' She took a sip of water as she felt a thickening in her throat. 'There certainly won't be any time to be shifting apartments.'

Finn nodded. There was no point reminding her that Isaac wasn't alone because he knew exactly how she felt. It felt wrong being away from him, leaving him in the care of strangers—no matter how excellent or vital it was.

He nodded. 'Okay, fine, but…' He put his hand into his pocket and pulled out a burgundy velvet box. 'I want you to have this.'

He opened it to reveal the one-carat princess-cut diamond—a princess for a princess. It sparkled in Pete's downlights as he pushed it across the table to her. 'I realised that I hadn't given you one yet and that was remiss of me. I want you to have it, to wear, so everyone knows we're going to be a family.'

Evie was rather pleased she wasn't drinking anything when he put the box on the table or she might well have choked to death this time. Her pulse thundered through her ears as she picked it up. The ring was exquisite in a platinum antique setting.

'It's beautiful,' she whispered. It was the kind of ring she would have picked out herself and just for a moment she wanted to hold it and look at it and marvel. 'It must have cost you a fortune.'

Finn shook his head. 'No price is too high for the mother of my child.'

Evie felt a hysterical sob rising in her throat and swallowed it down hard. Everything she had inside her wanted to take the exquisite piece of jewellery and put it on her finger and never take it off.

To be Finn's wife.

But she knew if she did, if she compromised what she needed from him, she'd lose herself for ever. With more self-control than she'd known she possessed, she snapped the lid shut and passed it back to him, keeping her gaze firmly fixed on the bead of moisture running down her glass. 'I'm not going to marry you, Finn.'

Finn frowned as a prickle of unease scratched at his hopes and dreams and he was reminded of how she hadn't been able to look at him yesterday. 'What?'

Evie fiddled with the straw in her glass. 'I know I told you I would but…that was before all of this.'

Finn put his hand over top of hers, stilling its swishing of the straw. 'Look at me, Evie,' he said.

Evie fleetingly thought of telling him to go to hell but this was a conversation that they might be better having now so Finn knew she couldn't be waited out, persuaded or bullied. So she looked at him and tried to keep the hurt from her gaze.

'What's really going on here?' he asked.

Evie sighed at the brilliant, clueless man in front of her. What would Lexi or Bella say to him? 'You suck at proposing, Finn.'

Finn snorted. She was having some kind of female hissy fit because he hadn't gone down on bended knee? 'I'm sorry I've been a little busy to organise a flash mob and a blimp.'

Evie felt tears well in her eyes and for an awful second she thought she was going to cry. Right here in the middle of Pete's. Wouldn't that be great for the gossips? 'I don't need grand gestures, Finn,' she said quietly. 'Not a flash mob or a blimp or even a bloody house. But I *do* need to hear three little words.' She paused and cleared her throat of its wobble. 'I'm not marrying you because you don't love me.'

Finn frowned. That was the most preposterous thing he'd ever heard. 'Yes, I do. Of course I do. I've told you that.' He had, hadn't he? More than once.

'Sure,' Evie said bitterly. 'Suddenly the

love is flooding in for Isaac so much it radiates out of you and you're dragging everything nearby with you like some bloody comet, and I've been swept up in it too.'

He shook his head. 'No, Evie, that's not right.'

'Isn't it?' she demanded in a loud, angry whisper, sitting forward in her chair. 'I'm the mother of your child—of course you love me, you have to. You've got me all set me up as this esteemed mother figure. As this revered nurturer. The provider of milk and changer of nappies.'

If Finn could have kicked his own butt he would have. 'Of course you mean more to me than that. I love *you*, Evie.'

Evie felt as if he'd struck her with the words, so obviously an afterthought. 'Then why in hell do I get a ring pushed across the table accompanied by a *This was remiss of me*. If you loved me, really loved me, as a woman, not just as the mother of your child, then you would have told me that. That's what men who love the women they propose to do. But you didn't. And do you know why?' she snarled, uncaring who might be overhearing their conversation, 'Because it never occurred to you. Because it's not the way you feel. Well, I'm sorry, Finn,' she said, standing up, not able to bear the look of total bewilderment on his face. 'I need more than that. I know that you had a terrible upbringing and you need a home and a family and you've got this whole fantasy going on around that, and I thought I could live with just that. But I can't. I won't.'

She sidestepped until she was out of the booth. 'Do me a favour, give me an hour with Isaac before you come back.'

And she whirled out of the pub before the first tear fell.

Lexi was alarmed when Evie arrived back with puffy eyes and insisted she'd ring her babysitter to stay longer, but Evie sent her on her way, assuring her she was fine, just Finn being Finn on top of the worry and stress over Isaac.

By the time Finn arrived back she had herself under control and was determined to stay that way. He looked at her tentatively and despite how he kept breaking her heart, she felt sorry for him. Finn was a man who'd shut himself down emotionally to deal with a crappy life. Opening up like this couldn't be easy for him.

'Evie, can we please talk—?'

Her quick, sharp headshake cut him off.

'Listen to me,' she said, her voice low so the nurse wasn't privy to their conversation. 'I do not want to talk about what happened today until after Isaac is home and we know he's safe and well. For the moment, for the foreseeable future, he is the *only* thing that's important. *The only thing that we talk about.* The only thing we concentrate on. *Just Isaac.*'

In the time she'd had to herself, looking down at the precious little bundle that connected her to Finn, Evie had decided she wasn't going to snivel about what had just happened. She'd drawn a line in the sand and that was her decision, and until Isaac was well enough to come home she wasn't going to think, cry or argue about it again.

'Can I have a commitment from you that you'll do the same?'

Finn opened his mouth to protest but Evie was looking so fierce and sure, and after the bungled way he'd managed the whole ring thing he wasn't keen to alienate her further. By his calculations, if everything went well Isaac would probably be discharged in a month or so once he hit a gestational age of around thirty-two weeks or a certain weight.

He could wait a month.

Live by her edict for another four weeks.

But after that she'd better prepare herself.

Because he intended to propose properly and leave her in absolutely no doubt of how much he loved her.

He nodded. 'Fine. But once Isaac is home, *we will be revisiting this, Evie.*'

Evie shivered at the steel in his tone and the flicker of blue flame in his eyes. 'Fine.'

Four days passed. Four days of tag-teaming, polite condition updates and stilted conversation. Evie taking the days, Finn the nights. Four days where Isaac continued to grow stronger and put on weight and have most of his lines removed and Evie was finally allowed to have her first kangaroo cuddle with him.

As she sat in the low comfy chair beside the cot, a squirmy, squeaky Isaac held upright against her naked chest, both of them wrapped up tight in a warm blanket, Evie wished Finn was there. The nurse took a picture but it wasn't quite the same thing. This was the kind of moment that parents should share, watching their tiny premmie baby snuffling and miraculously rooting around for a nipple, even finding it and trying to suckle, no matter how weakly.

She felt teary but determinedly pushed them away. She'd been strong and true to her promise not to dwell on it—stress and exhaustion helping—and she wouldn't do it now, not during this simply amazing moment when she and her baby bonded, skin on skin.

On the fifth morning Evie woke early and couldn't go back to sleep, trying to decide if Finn would mind having his time cut short. Or at least sharing a bit of it with her. It made sense to go in—all she was doing was lying there thinking about Isaac anyway and she could feel her breasts were full.

May as well head to the hospital and pump.

Evie was being buzzed in through the main entry doors half an hour later. She noticed a group of nurses standing off to one side of the station and frowned. She smiled at them as she went past and they smiled back, indicating for her to hush and stay with them for a moment. Bemused, Evie turned to see what had them so agog. Her smile slipped as she realised they were watching Finn kangaroo-cuddling with Isaac through the isolation room's windows.

It was a touching, tender moment, stealing her breath and rendering her temporarily paralysed.

Her two darling boys.

'The great Finn Kennedy,' one nurse whispered.

'Who'd have thunk?' said another.

Evie left them to their amazement. Not that she could blame them. She doubted anyone, Finn included, would have ever thought he could be brought to his knees by a tiny baby.

She stood in the doorway for a moment, just admiring them from the back. Finn sitting in the low chair next to the cot, obviously shirtless if the bare shoulder blade just visible through the folds of the blanket was any indication, skin on skin with his son.

She swallowed hard against the lump in her throat, preparing to enter. But then she realised that Finn was talking quietly to Isaac and she hung back, not wanting to intrude on a father-son moment.

'There we are,' Finn said, 'I think we've got you comfortable now you've realised no matter how much you look for it, I'm just not your mummy. She'll be along later. She won't really talk to me because she's mad at me and she'll only have eyes for you anyway.'

Evie's ears pricked up at the conversation and she leaned in a little.

'My fault, I'm afraid, little mate. Totally stuffed everything up there. Take it from me, women may be complicated but in the end all they really want is for you to love them. I've never been good at that stuff, couldn't even tell your uncle Isaac I loved him until he was dying in my arms. You're a lot like him and I promise I'm going to tell you every day. And hopefully I'll get a chance to tell your mum as well. Trust me on this, matey, never make *I love you* sound like an afterthought. Stupid, stupid, stupid.'

Evie held her breath.

'And now she thinks I only love her because she's part of some package deal with you. That I only see her as *your* mother. And I can't tell her she's wrong, that's she's the sexiest, smartest woman I've ever met and I'm crazy about her because I promised her I wouldn't talk about it until you were home. So you need to hurry up and get home, you hear?'

Evie blinked back a threatening tear as she listened unashamedly now.

'Because the truth is I don't want to live a day of my life without her in it. I love you, little guy, and the same applies to you, but it's different with your mother. I want to hold her and touch her and kiss her and make love with her and do all those things that people in love do. You probably won't ever realise this because she's your mum, but she's one sexy lady.'

Evie blushed at the rumble in Finn's voice.

'And of course I love her because she's your mother and there are things she can give you that I can't, but I love her also because she can give *me* things that you can't— a different kind of love. And I never thought I'd hear myself say this but I need that. And I want to give her the love that you can't. I want to love her like a woman deserves to be loved. And I never want to stop.'

Evie let the tears come this time. She didn't try to stop them. She pushed off the doorframe and was at his side in five seconds. Bending her head and kissing him two seconds after that.

'Why,' she demanded face wet, eyes glistening, 'didn't you say those things in Pete's?'

Finn looked into her beautiful, interesting face made even more so by two wet tear tracks, his heart thudding in his chest. 'Because I'm emotionally stunted and incredibly stupid.'

She laughed and kissed him again. 'Do you really mean all those things? About loving me as a woman, not just as Isaac's mother?'

Finn smiled. 'Of course. You wouldn't let me tell you so I figured I'd tell him.'

Evie crouched beside him, peeking inside the blanket at Isaac snuggled up in a little ball against Finn's chest. 'I'm glad you did.'

'So am I,' Finn murmured, looking down into her face. 'I'm just sorry I got it so wrong for so long, Evie. I *do* love you. Just as you are. Evie Lockheart. No one's mother or sister or doctor. Just you. You helped me love again, feel again, and I need you in my life. All of you.'

Evie nodded, two more tears joining the others. 'And I love you.'

Finn dropped a kiss on her mouth and it was the sweetest thing Evie had ever known.

'Don't think you're off the hook for the flash mob and the blimp, though,' she warned as they broke apart.

Finn grinned. 'I'll consider myself on notice.'

And then a tiny little snuffly sneeze came from under the covers and they smiled at each other, brimming with love.

EPILOGUE

EVIE LOOKED UP from watching Isaac happily crawling around the back yard to see her husband approaching with a massive wrapped box.

Finn grimaced as he set the heavy box on the ground. 'Delivery for the birthday boy.'

Isaac turned at the interesting new arrival and crawled their way, gurgling happily. It was hard to believe a year had passed since the frantic night of his birth and while the doctors still corrected his age to nine months, it was still his *birth* day.

His milestones were behind, he was only just crawling and he was smaller than most kids his age, but he was bright and engaging and his parents were besotted with him.

Finn bent and picked his son up off the grass, kissing him on the head. 'What do you think about that?' he asked him.

Isaac kicked his legs excitedly and Finn

and Evie laughed as they helped him pull the paper off the box and get it open. Inside sat the most exquisitely carved and decorated rocking horse Evie had ever seen.

'Finn,' she breathed reverently as he pulled it out and placed it on the grass. 'It's beautiful... Where did you get it?'

Isaac squirmed to get down and Finn obliged. 'It's not from me,' he murmured, upending the box and searching for a card. A piece of thick embossed card slipped out.

Finn read it. 'It's from Khalid,' he murmured.

Evie stared at it. A Saudi oil prince had sent Isaac a first birthday present. The sun shone down on the exquisite workmanship and they both admired it for a moment.

'Is that...gold leaf?' she asked.

Finn nodded. 'I think so.'

They looked at each other and laughed. Then they heard Isaac giggling too and looked down to find him peeking out of the box at them.

'But who needs gold leaf when you've got a box?' Finn smiled.

And Evie watched with joy and love in her heart as Finn pushed a giggling Isaac round and round the yard in his cardboard car.

* * * * *